EASTON ESTATE

D.R.L. Hicks

ISBN: 9798685764904

Cover design by: D.R.L. Hicks
Printed in the United States of America

"Ignorance is bliss. Bliss is a perception—not reality."

CHAPTER 1: FIRST NIGHT

I, Henry Torrington, made a dumb decision. I should have just gone to bed.

The situation: after a hard day's work, those moving boxes don't move themselves, I decided to watch some TV in the new house. Correction: the only "new" aspect of this place is the boxes I lugged around and my arrival. The "new home" my parents picked out is at least a century old and does nothing to mask that aging rot. How did the realtor describe it? Right, he claimed, "... run-down—a fixer-upper." Liar. "A drafty ruin" is a better description.

Whatever. After hours of moving boxes, I am sore, tired, strained and exhausted. Sleep should come easy in this condition. But no, I decided some TV would help me relax. Plus, I needed the reward. That and I went through all the trouble to get the cables hooked up right—so many tangles. A cruel twist of fate almost wasted my efforts—the service provider hasn't come through. That means no cable or dish—whatever Mom and Dad picked, or internet yet. I am cut off from the outside world. It just leaves just the local freebie channels. I should have seen that coming.

I hooked up the DVD player, but of course, I can't find any of our DVDs. Some luck came through for me though. One of the local channels was running something decent. The station ran a horror movie marathon. It is strange though; Halloween is almost six months away. I don't associate late spring with horror, but I can't complain. Something to watch is better than nothing.

So I had thought.

All this led to my second mistake. The first was not just going straight to bed. Then, I figured a little horror wouldn't scare me. I'd seen a bunch with friends back home in Georgia. Turns out horror watched in a real old house, alone, and in the creepy basement ratchets up the experience to a whole new level.

I swear I heard mumbling. It wasn't coming from the speaker system. It had to have come from behind the wall at one point. Our surround sound can't be that good. Or maybe it is? I am tired and with those movies running, my imagination is definitely awake. The whole sound system works—I followed instructions when I set it up. I was more with it then.

Anyways, old houses settle in the most disturbing ways at night. I continued to watch film after film. That was the third mistake—the binging. There was a marathon's worth. Minutes must have become hours. No commercials either, it was just one movie after another without interruption. I was immersed. Though I can't remember what all I watched. I only turned it off now because the next one was a film I'd seen before and didn't care to see again. It sucked the first time I saw it. Why repeat it unless you have no choice?

So, I've escaped the glowing abyss of the TV. All that's left now is to navigate one creepy and unfamiliar horror house in near total darkness. I'd stay in the basement. However, aside from my addition of the media center, the rest of the room looks like a dungeon. In this paranoid state, a dark, underground confined space serves as a strong sleep distraction. Despite that fact, I am certain I dozed off a few times. I don't remember starting or finishing one or two of the movies in the marathon.

Dragging my limbs, my muscles ache from all those boxes. I guess I did not lift properly with my legs. My arms are sore. I can feel every muscle strained in my back. Stairs aren't helping—physically or audibly. Each worn wooden step creaks with a sound best compared to the planks of an old, rotted rope bridge across a cliff. I could wake the dead with the creaking of these old steps. Climbing out of the basement, I think I hear an old clock chime. It sounds like I guess it's coming from the living room? Strange. I figured that clock wouldn't tick without serious repairs and a deep cleaning. I can't imagine how much dust buildup this place has had.

Pressing on, I reach the ground floor. Halfway there. My room is on the second floor. Before heading upstairs, I decide to check the front door. After all, I am home alone. Mom and Dad trusted me to arrive first. They still have some business to tend to back South before joining me up here in the boonies.

Ah, I can check off another mistake. Looking outside reminds me of another detail about the property. I was trying to ignore it. I'd almost even forgotten about it too. This old house is smack dab in the middle of the woods. The realtor wasn't lying this time, claiming it's "an old house in the country." I'm a city slicker—I know it and won't deny it. There's no light out there—just shadows of trees and who knows what else. At least this door has a lot of locks I can set.

Now as I turn from the front door. I really ought to check the doors in the kitchen and back hall. Though I haven't used those yet. They should still be locked from who knows when. I suppose locked by whoever owned this ruin last. I'll skip them. Let's get some rest.

I don't even bother with the lights. The chandelier lighting the grand staircase likes to do this annoying flickering trick when you're halfway up. Who knows what afterimage I'd see in this sleep deprived state? Anyways, this is probably one of the smarter things I have accomplished. Though only using the moonlight from the windows is stupid. So, I guess I break even.

The handrail proves useful and I continue to use it to navigate the second floor part that overlooks the entry. The rail is worn, but smooth—it has handled ag—ow. Never mind. Splinters. There's a rough patch. I guess that's another reason why this is a "fixer-upper." Though lighting is poor, I didn't get anything major. Pulling out the fine sliver out—I'm fine.

Before turning down a short hall to my room, I look back down on the entry. There's a faint glow somewhere below from, I guess the music room? I must have left something on. I wonder what it is? Oh well, I'm too tired to feed my curiosity. I'll pass on checking it out right now.

Reaching my room, I find my bed and fall onto it, ready to sleep now.

I think I hear something—piano music? No, that must be the house settling. I'm too tired to check.

CHAPTER 2: SECOND DAY

Oh god. I open my eyes. An all-body ache hits me before I can even clear the fog of sleep. No, that was a complete knockout. I was out cold. Yesterday's strain is today's soreness. Now, I just lay here. At least I left my bed clear. I passed out on it. Fully dressed, without even bothering with the sheets.

From my sprawled-out position, I take stock of things. Most of the boxes in my bedroom sit unopened. Fortunately, this is a decent-sized room, so I can rearrange furniture. Still however, I'll need help to get that desk in. Cobwebs in the corners—that's another thing to take care of on the growing mental list. I can't help but sigh. This is a lot of work! Mom and Dad owe me big.

I draw a bit of strength and dig my cellphone out of my pocket. It's the only working clock in the house. Already afternoon, apparently, it's almost one. Well, I guess I'll take lunch to start the day.

Also, there's a message. Checking my missed call, I see it's from Mom. She called this morning at 10. I must have really been out of if to miss my ringtone. The voicemail is about what I expect. They are checking up on me. I called when I first arrived. Not much has changed except now I know they can't organize well when packing. Calling back, I am forced to leave a voicemail. They're busy too. Plus, I think they are several time zones over. Coordinating might be tricky.

Well, I need to get going if I'm going to get something to eat before dinner. I roll over—and out! Falling off the bed. Ow. I can feel the bare hardwood flooring. It's very hard, as the name suggested.

Picking myself up and dusting off, I head for the kitchen. I guess this place has an old European-ish grandeur to it. My door leads out to a railing that looks down on the entry. I suppose the entry would be classier if it didn't have boxes and furniture stacked all over. Oh, and this place needs a lot of work. Dust, cobwebs, dirt, touches of water damage—this is a real "project house."

My path down is by way of the grand staircase, through the hall and to the kitchen in the back corner of the house. This place is large and feels even larger since I'm alone here. The kitchen isn't unpacked, but at least it's clean. Entirely through my efforts, of course. It's one reason more isn't done around here. Our move was messy. The biggest fault with Mom and Dad is their consistent mislabeling of almost all the boxes. I didn't have the movers around long enough to open boxes and help me get everything put in its proper place.

On move-in day, I ate pizza for lunch and dinner and left no leftovers. I have to check if the refrigerator is down to the correct temperature.

My god, what is that smell?! The stench from opening the sealed door rolls out. Survival reflexes make me slam it shut quick! Utterly disgusting! There was no food beyond some leftover Chinese boxes spilled out in there. When did we have that? That noxious odor, it means it's got some strange growth! It must, ew, that's from before the move.

So then, lunch out today. I gag realizing that was in the fridge on the drive up here! Halfway across the country! Note to self, add finding the mini fridge to "Need to Find" list. It will have to serve for all food storage until I clean that toxic waste dump out.

New plan, I'll go into town, there I can dodge food poisoning as a death. Town is close anyways, despite the woods hiding it. No matter what though, I need to go into town since I can't find the coffeemaker. I need caffeine before I can feel halfway human.

An awful smell persists. Oh, that's me. A shower first, then a change of clothes. I can't have a bad impression for my first trip into town.

* * *

Ah, I feel better. Still there's an ache from yesterday's work and today's tumble out of bed, but the hot shower helped. From my duffle bag, I rooted out a clean pair of jeans. It's still chilly here out west, in spite of it being almost May! I also found a blue and orange polo. Rumors say this town is more dressed up. But I'm a teen. Which, I think, should exempt me. I grab sneakers and a ball cap. Finally, being a Broncos fan should be acceptable in this part of the country.

Ready to seize what's left of the day, or at least get food and caffeine, I head out. Leaving the house gives me the feeling of wealth and power. I saw what we paid for the property. It cost a fourth of our first, smaller home, which was in the nice part of suburbia near Atlanta. It was nothing fancy, but certainly an upgrade from an apartment. They built this house to show off and entertain the rich and famous. Or at least whoever came close to that this far out in the sticks. The nearest city of real note is six hours or so away and two states south.

Outside, I grab my bike and pedal out. Though close to town, a pine forest wraps around the house. And the town too is set deep into this forest. The nearest paved road is down a dirt path. Civilization apparently never developed out this direction. There's not much undergrowth, just some moss-covered rocks amongst evergreens. Hilly too, I have to shift gears. I'm not too particularly rushed, but I have never ridden a bike on a dirt road this far. I guess this makes up for all the "nature stuff" I missed in my childhood. I've never done any serious time out alone in forests, never camped, or hiked for more than a couple hours. To think, I used to imagine "nature" as involving an annual trip to a nearby state park.

The first part of town is the cemetery. It runs alongside of the dirt road that is practically our driveway. I guess that since this road leads only to my house, I have a graveyard as part of the front. That's a morbid realization. It's an old one too. The markers look worn as seen through the rusting wrought-iron fence topped with barbed wire. Out of habit, I check the top of the fence. I once heard a story that the direction of the barbs tells a lot about the place. If the barbs face out, it is to deter grave robbers and troublemakers from disturbing the city of the dead. If they point inwards, they contain something sinister within.

Here? They face both directions: inwards and outwards. I hope that's just a tall tale then.

I soon reach the paved road. If I recall my instructions, I just need to follow the cemetery fence and I'll eventually run into the town. A bike path runs alongside the road and cemetery. That's convenient.

As I reach the end of the cemetery, I come to a church. The map I think called it, "Memorial Chapel." It's an old stone structure with a yard lined with a whole bunch of flags and statues. I only recognize the American flag and the state flag—that's thanks to geography class. A bunch of Europeans originally settled the town, so I guess most of them are foreign countries. Hunger doesn't allow this odd sight to hold me though, and I keep pedaling along. I live here now. I can check into it later. Across the street is a small park put into a hillside. Given its early afternoon and that school is still in session here, the playground is naturally empty at this hour. Everything is well-kept, but empty. It's eerie in a post-apocalyptic sort of way.

At last, people! Downtown almost instantly appears as I round the bend of a hill. Surprisingly, I come to an area it's quite built up. It's like an island of civilization in a sea of forest. Though nothing looks to be of this century. Nothing looks to even to be from even before the 1950s. I don't know architecture, but I know old when I see it. Here has an "Old World" look to it. It's like out of a movie. The streets are paved with bricks and the shops are on the lower half of the buildings. Well-dressed people are busy moving about. I guess on some late lunch break errands.

I can explore town later. Lunch and caffeine, preferably together, is in first order. There's a restaurant with some outdoor seating nearby. It's over near a grassy square with a woman's statue in the middle. The sign calls the place *Kaffeehaus Neu Welt*. It looks promising. On the sign is a coffee cup and globe. I think that means coffee at least. I have two semesters of Spanish under my belt. So far—not helping. Oh well. I head over there and lock my bike on a rack near the door. This town does have a certain convenience with its charm.

The smells of coffee and a busy kitchen fill my nose as I enter. Inside I find a cavernous sunken café animated by light chatter and a piano skillfully played in the corner. Tables and booths are amongst pillars that support the ceiling. Said ceiling is painted with I guess scenes of the Dakotas. There's prairie and hill scenes with Indians, cowboys and settlers—like out of the history books. The lighting is dimmed, creating a cozy feel.

A sign reads, "Seat Yourself." Ah, but where can I sit? Scanning the crowded room, I see no open tables. Also, no free stools at the bar.

I manage to make eye contact with someone in a booth towards the back of the room. He waves to me, gesturing to come over. It's a guy about my age. He's white and maybe slightly taller than average. Dressed in some sort of school uniform with a light blue blazer, he must be a student enjoying some sort of open campus policy. As I approach, I see he is at work. Next to him is his backpack, and half the table is covered with books and notes. He appears to be writing a letter. Going by the English-French dictionary, I'd venture to guess French homework.

"You can sit here. I won't be here much longer," he tells me, as I get closer.

"Thanks," I reply and accept the offer. I can't help but offer the comment, "Busy place."

"It is the place to be at this hour. People need to re-caffeinate around this time," he muses while raising his own nearly drained mug.

Before we can exchange another word, a waitress appears. Dressed in a black dress with a white apron, she appears to have stepped out of another era. "Can I take your order, sir?" she asks. The waitress even sounds a bit foreign with an accent.

"Ah, it is my first time here," I admit. She immediately pulls out a menu from an apron pocket.

Handing me a menu card, she recommends, "In no offense sir, you look like you need at least a double espresso. It's not much liquid, but the caffeine looks to be your main interest," she is an angel.

"Yes, I'll need that to start then."

"Right away sir," she then departs.

I take a look at the menu. They mostly do breakfast, coffee and desserts. Oh, the lunch special is a Reuben sandwich. I like those.

Satisfied that I know what I want, I set the menu down. Looking to the person across from me, he seems to be wrapping up a letter with a signature. His handwriting is an elaborate cursive I can't read upside down.

As he folds his letter he explains, "A letter for my pen pal." He sticks it in an addressed air mail envelope and seals it. Satisfied with finishing the task, he looks to me and asks, "So are you traveling or a new resident?"

"New in town. I moved into the house out past the cemetery," I answer him.

"Ah," he pauses as if reluctant and then adds, "The old Easton Estate. It was once a grand place, a very, very long time ago."

"Certainly, it needs a major fix up now," I admit. The house is old. But oddly enough, it has updated modern features in spite of its run-down state.

The waitress returns with my coffee and a glass of water. I take this time to order and she departs again. Taking a sip of my coffee, I feel the bitter taste surge through my veins. Ah, I needed that!

"You look quite tired," he comments. He is perceptive, like the waitress. Granted, I wasn't trying to hide it.

"Moving takes a lot of energy. It was a first day with a whirlwind of boxes. Then I got caught up in the horror film marathon and stayed up way too late." I reply.

He seems to know something. His eyes don't hide that at all. But he tells me, "Well, I'd like to hear more, but I have afternoon classes. I don't want to lose my off-campus privileges."

"Of course," I tell him. It sounds like a nice school.

As he packs his things, he tells me, "If you have time later today, we could meet up after school and I could show you around town if you're interested."

"Would tomorrow work? I have errands I have to run later today," like groceries.

He thinks for a second before answering, "We could meet at 12 for lunch over at Carsen's Café. It has a larger- lunch menu. Then I could give you a driving tour of the town. I don't have classes as late tomorrow afternoon."

"Sure, where's that?" I ask.

"Opposite side of this square," he answers, gesturing outside. Fully packed up, he bids me, "Until later."

"Yeah, goodbye," I bid him back as he heads for the register.

Only as he heads out, I realize we never exchanged names. He seemed to be in a rush though.

Oh well.

The waitress is coming back. My food is here and that requires my full attention. I have plenty of time to meet new people in this place.

CHAPTER 3: SECOND NIGHT

Grocery shopping with a bike is a pain in the ass. Normally, Mom or Dad would drive *the car* and I would tag along as a bag boy. This now is more than a chore, especially in an unfamiliar store. Sure, the selection wasn't big, but still I don't know where anything is and there's nothing in the house.

Plus, the store was on the opposite side of town. I took the streetcar as much as possible, but that only got me as far as the chapel. I still had to pedal past the cemetery and up the long, long dirt road. Out here, I need a car. The other struggle was loading things on the bike. It has a rack and straps—I got lucky that nothing fell off! I'm actually old enough to drive in this state too. There could be some benefits to living in "the sticks" once I'm actually settled in.

Dinner was steak on the grill. The kitchen stove is a gas one, and I don't know if it's turned on yet. Plus, I don't know when it was last used. Given the house's age, that question might be answered in decades. Plus, I know how to use a propane grill without an explosion risk.

The cuts of meat are cheap, but steak sauce helped. I served them with a baked potato on the grill and an apple. A sack of apples is a pain to haul by bicycle, but easy to prepare—good thing the water is turned on. I ate well. Though our steak knives are ridiculously dull.

Sore legs make me not inclined to go upstairs, so I will take advantage of the living room couch. A nap is now in order.

* * *

I awake to hear the ticking of the grandfather clock. It came with the house. We never owned such an annoying thing before. I wasn't aware it even worked. How do you even set it? Did the realtor do that? No, I don't remember hearing the clock's ticking during the day. Getting up, I go over to inspect the ancient thing.

Despite the rest of the house being worn and beaten, the clock is in excellent condition. Gold hands show the hour to be 11, the minute and secondhand race for midnight with a constant tick-tock. The face also tracks the phases of the moon and year. The main face—it's a century off though. All the hands soon converge on the 12 and the bells within it chime the midnight hour.

Well, that happened.

I hear something other than the clock ticking. It's muffled, coming from—upstairs? Maybe voices? That's what it sounds like. Weird. Did I leave something on upstairs? I played some music when I was working.

I think I had left something on upstairs—or was it downstairs? Now I cannot remember where. The sounds right now are distinctly upstairs. The stereo's battery should have died hours ago if that's the case. And I still can't find the power cord., Although wherever it was, I should have noticed sooner. Why now, at midnight no less? I'm not crazy, I can still hear it. Plus, I am wide awake now.

My nap restored some strength, so I'll check it out at the source. As I take the grand staircase, I think I am able to pinpoint the noises. It sounds like it comes from the, what was it called? The parlor, that's it. Now those are definitely human voices. Probably two—one male, another female. But how? I didn't have any music like that. Is someone here? No. I am home alone...so is it a radio? I can't recall if my stereo has that feature. We have a portable radio somewhere in one of these boxes. I bet there're batteries still in it. Batteries are something we'd forget to remove in the move.

I don't know what's going on in there. Nevertheless, I intend to find out. As I reach the top of the staircase, the hairs on the back of my neck stand on end. This chill peaks as I reach for the double doors. I plan to throw them open dramatically. An electric current practically runs through me when I put my hands on the old gilded knobs. The voices are indiscernible, but they sound human. What, what else could they be? And they grow louder, still though I can't make out a single word.

Now! I throw open the doors!

Two figures face each other in the center of the room. My entry draws their attention. I can't get a closer look. The pale forms in the dark room lunge towards me in a rush! They send boxes and furniture flying!

Something rams into me and I fall down! It is cold—I feel like a livewire doused in ice! A mash of colors fills my vision and there's awful screeching. Then darkness—

*　*　*

The clock chimes another hour. The sound! I am wide awake now! And my head hurts. Did I black out? My whole body is sore from falling on the hardwood floor.

Mentally, I try to piece together what just happened. It was all just a blur of colors before darkness. Digging out my cellphone it is—1:20 AM. Right, I was before the grandfather clock and heard noises upstairs. That was around midnight! I investigated, saw something, and was knocked out by something. Was all that imagination? Right, whatever rushed me knocked over a bunch of things in the parlor!

I sit up. Ow, ow. The doors to the parlor are closed. The clock still ticks below. I think I am hearing piano music too.

Strange. Hearing music, fainting at the top of the stairs, and possibly seeing things. Just what exactly is going on here?

Feeling tired, I close my eyes. What is that sound? Is that a piano? So, there's music coming from downstairs. I just now noticed that. This is all madness! I shouldn't be home alone! Sitting there at the top of the stairs, I listen to the slow, sad song. The more I listen, the more depressing I find the tune. I am too exhausted to move from this spot...

CHAPTER 4: THIRD DAY

Ghosts!

This is my first thought before I can even open my eyes. Did I just have a close encounter with something supernatural? I don't know. Or was it a nightmare? I just don't know.

Opening my eyes, I see I am still in yesterday's clothes. Sitting up, I find myself on the floor before the parlor door. I'm lucky I didn't tumble down the main staircase. Just a roll over, mere inches, and in my sleep could have broken my back!

The doors to the parlor are closed. So, some parts of what happened I think are true. I did pass out at the top of the stairs and I do remember checking on noises up here. Now I need to confirm the last bit—that supernatural encounter. I know I didn't get far enough in to damage anything in there.

Getting up, I am reminded that hardwood flooring is not a good sleeping surface. I guess now I know how old people feel. I stretch and pop a few stiff joints. This is really just stalling.

If the house is haunted, well, countless issues inevitably arise. Exhaustion and moving stress are driving me to pass out on the top of the stairs and hallucinate. Going crazy can't be healthy. I check the clock on my cellphone. Maybe that guy at the coffee shop can help me or least knows something. I need to get going if I want to make lunch. Let's get this check over with.

I open the doors to the parlor. Boxes and furniture lay knocked aside in a path that seems to come from where I recall the two figures were arguing. Somewhere in the center of the room. But I thought ghosts were intangible? Unless it was a poltergeist—they're ones that chuck stuff around. That or I imagined it. Maybe an animal? This house is in the middle of the woods. However, I locked my doors. Heck one of them doesn't even open! I know all the windows are closed as well. I inspected all of them myself. Though I don't know of any other major openings. I suppose I could have done this through sleepwalking. I have never slept walk before though. But even in the unlikely case I did, I should have some bruises from knocking around these objects. The furniture is rather hard.

Well, I'll sort out this mess later. Right now, I need to get ready and get going. The bike ride will be tough in my tired and sore state. So, first, I need to change clothes. As I head for my bedroom, I note that I cannot hear the clock downstairs anymore. I'll check it when I get down there, I could have sworn I heard it last night.

Dressed and downstairs, I now double-check the grandfather clock. It's not working right now. Strange, was it my imagination? Grabbing a pen and piece of notebook paper out of a nearby box, I tear the page in half. I write the exact time on the still face of the dead clock on both halves. The clock reads 12:00 on April 31, 1907. Also, the moon phase dial is broken. Though, the twisted needle points to a full moon. I put one-half of the paper into my pocket and the other in a box by the door filled with, oh, so that's where the computer printer went.

Anyways, I'm ready. So, I set off. Had I been thinking I would have had the guy come get me with his car. Oh well, biking should clear my head of this craziness.

❋ ❋ ❋

Carsen's Café is right out of that iconic part of the 1950s. Though set in some old world looking building, the interior is the chrome-lined and red plush booth-filled expression of Americana. I got here first surprisingly. So, to pass the time, I ordered coffee. It comes in a thick-walled mug from a stereotypical glass pot. It's not espresso, but a pot of the good old diner coffee will do the trick. This should tide me over until the burger and fries arrive. I feel so cliched. It's like being in a movie.

Just as I start on my first cup, he arrives. I don't have his name. Entering, he immediately finds me in the busy lunch crowd. He signals to the counter worker with a wave. The employee merely adjusts his paper diner hat in reply.

Joining me without greeting, he immediately asks, "How is the estate?"

"My parents don't know how to label boxes, so that alone makes things a mess. Further, being alone up there is either driving me crazy or the place is haunted," I answer.

He blinks and gives me a critical stare. What is he calculating? It only passes for a second or two before he admits, "Well, the house is haunted."

A waiter brings a mug and pours him a cup of coffee. He makes his coffee with cream and sugar, leaving me to stew on that statement.

I admit, "There's a man and woman. I have had the misfortune of meeting them in the parlor. And, I think there might be one more, a piano player."

He nods, seeming to be lost in thought.

Okay this is strange. I have to ask, "Isn't this the part where you tell me about the ghosts?"

"I don't know if I should. Do you believe in that kind of thing?" he asks.

Ah, I can reason this out, "You're worried about that, 'power of suggestion' thing. If you tell me, it will fill me with thoughts of paranoia, and make a self-fulfilling prophecy."

"Well, somewhat correct, but you know the saying, 'Ignorance is bliss?'" he comes back.

Point taken, but "Bliss is a perception—not the reality of

the situation."

"Touché. Shall I enlighten you? Or well, I guess burden you? If you find it comes off as demolishing bliss," he asks.

"Tell me," I get to the point. Our food then arrives, so I add, "In a minute, I am starving." I haven't eaten since yesterday's steak. Getting here has made me hungry.

After a few bites of an excellent meal, he launches into detail, "The Easton Estate is haunted by the original residents of the house, the Easton family. They died practically a century ago. Since then anyone else who has tried to live there has either died or fled before the week's end."

"I presume survivors were scared off?" I have to ask.

"Enough of them. Most gave up by the fourth night. Only a few residents held out, they were usually found dead or hopelessly insane by a week's end."

"Those not scared off, how did they die?" I want details and this guy seems knowledgeable.

"Are you sure you want to learn this over lunch?" he asks, clearly it is for my sake, because he continues to enjoy his meal.

"I was a lifeguard. I have seen some nasty accidents and even had to clean up a few," I tell him. I don't envy anyone listening in though.

"Most mimic how the first owners went. Mrs. Easton was hanged from the entry mezzanine and the husband was shot in the library. Their daughter stabbed with a trail of blood tracing from the kitchen to the conservatory. Most deaths following the original tragedy oddly involved strangulation by rope or being shot. Though, stabbings are rare." he explains.

"I was expecting details," I am unsurprised. His statement doesn't require a preface. The news describes and shows worse.

"Alright," he answers before a few bites. He seems to prepare himself but notices something behind me. I look, the worker at the counter does not look happy. He glares at our table.

Turning back around he tells me, "I won't go into graphic detail in consideration for the lunch crowd. Rather, anyways, the statistics are more disturbing. The first couple to move in after the Eastons went mad and were institutionalized back east in Yankton. Nobody ever got a coherent story out of them. They lasted the longest at a full six nights."

After a pause, he continues, "Between the wars, a family of seven all died on the fourth night. During the Second World War, the government tried to keep POWs there. They and their guards all went mad or died. Those exact numbers are still classified. About three teens died there in the 50s, well officially, they committed suicide. At least one family has tried living there almost every year from 1970 until 1985. People kept coming because the house is such a good deal even for this area."

I nod at that last point. The place was absurdly cheap. He then concludes, "However, survivors of the house have turned up at the hospital with gunshot wounds, bruises and strangulation marks. The Investigator's Society of Supernatural Phenomena conducted a stay there about a year ago. We barely made out alive on the fourth night."

He stops nervously. I glance around. People are trying very hard to ignore or shoot us harsh looks. "Sorry, that's a lot to process," I reply. Of course, this begs the question, "How does such a house remain standing after so much tragedy?"

"The stories weren't gathered in one place until last year with the publication of the Society's findings. It was just the creepy house—one knew the numbers. Then the house sold to your family before anyone could intervene," he replies.

"The Investigator's Society of—it was—of Supernatural Phenomena?" I find that to be a mouthful.

"Yes, it was a high school club. I was in it in my freshmen year. We conducted a study of supernatural occurrences in the Black Hills area. The book we published, and the risks taken to gather information forced the Society to disband," he explains.

His gaze is distant, looking past me as he speaks. As if he has seen things. I can only imagine what he and his group saw.

Before I can ask which part he contributed to, a cellphone rings. He digs out a bulky flip phone while commenting, "Excuse me, that's probably my sister. She wanted to join us on the tour and has the jeep. He answers, "Hello?" His expression shows that he was not expecting any calls.

I can't hear what's going on, but it cannot be good. Our conversation has put a strain in his expression. But the cellphone conversation causes his face to lose all color. He replies after a moment, "I…I see. Al-alright, I am—I'm still at the diner. Yes. Okay, bye."

He hangs up and says to me, "I can't give you the tour today. There's been, well, there's been a family emergency. I'm afraid I'll be gone a few days."

"That's no problem for me. May I ask what happened?"

"I don't have the exact details. It deals with my cousin down in Colorado. My sister and I are heading down right away," as he talks, he starts digging out his wallet.

"I see, well, I hope it all goes well," what else can I say?

"Well, if you are like the rest this may be the last I see of you…dead or alive," he muses as he shakily counts out the amount he owes.

"I'll be careful. There's a book, right? I'll get that," I assure him, "You worry about your family." This doesn't feel like a final meeting,

"Well, alright. In my family they say, '*Family is foundation*,'" he seems to say that more for himself than me. Then he recommends to me, "There's a bookstore one block over. There's a map out front that points it out."

"Alright, thanks," I reply.

"Right," he says as he looks out the window for his ride, "Oh and tell them, 'the Society sent me.' That's the phrase. And there's my ride. Goodbye and good luck," he bids me as he gets up.

"You too," I wish him back. It is a strained farewell.

He heads for the counter, pays and then leaves on a light blue jeep that pulls up out front. I look at my half-eaten lunch. Strangely, I don't feel like finishing. The tensions spoiled this meal.

* * *

Post lunch, my next stop is obvious—to the bookstore. I haven't really been to one for a while. I am more of a movie guy.

The towering building of *Lorraine and Daughters Book Emporium* occupies a whole block. Inside are tons of shelves, all which overflow with books. I have never seen so many before. And the place screams utter chaos. It's as if somebody mistook an Escher painting as a floorplan.

Luckily, the front desk is dead ahead. An older woman, perhaps ironically reading an eBook, staffs it. She sees me approach greets me saying, "Good afternoon young sir. What can we do for you?"

"Hello, I need a book put out by the Investigator's Society of Supernatural Phenomena. I was told to say the 'Society sent me.'"

"New resident?"

"Son of the new owners of the Easton Estate, I am Henry Torrington," I introduce myself as I reach the wooden desk overcrowded with books.

"Well, I don't envy you. That house is cursed. The damned specters locked in there make it a suburb of hell come nighttime," she says before crossing herself.

"I've been there two days. Does it really live up to its reputation?" The story, now that I've had a moment to think with the walk here, sounds a bit outlandish. This could be small town amusement and my sleep deprivation at play.

"Well, 'believe what you will,' that's what people say these days. However, the statistics add up correctly," she pulls out a gray cloth bound hardcover book. In gold lettering its cover reads the title: *The Paranormal, Supernatural, and Cryptozoological Report of the Black Hills.* It appears to bear the seal of the Society: a magnify glass crossed over a bug net in an oval. Around the seal reads: *To seek that which dwells just beyond the mundane world.*

"Wow, this was produced by high school students?" I feel inadequate.

"They were a school club of ten students with a drive to consolidate the tall tales, ghost stories and outlandish claims of this region. Their lazy advisor, he lost his job. He gave them a letter of introduction endorsed by the school. The Society then used it to access everything from private properties, an abandoned mineshaft and of course that house. Also, they got into police reports as well as municipal, state and national archives, etc."

"So, they were disbanded because they took immense risks?" I surmise as I pick up the book. Flipping through it, I find it has footnotes—this is extensive.

"They ran their research almost entirely in secret. Funded their expeditions through fundraisers and key sponsorships with various local companies and tourism bureaus. Though after publication their school disbanded them. The Society's claims aren't what bother people, it's the fact that children went on dangerous expeditions to find out," she explains.

"Are the contents all true?" I have to ask. All I am hearing is a description of a bunch of teens who figured out how to take risks on another's dime. I flip to the front and find the book is signed: *Free to the inhabitants of the Easton Estate. May Time be ever at your side.* Ten signatures and a stamp of the seal of the Society follow this.

"Depends on the section. I grew up in this town and I believe something foul is at work there. That was all even before their efforts. If you seek facts, the Easton Estate is the most thoroughly researched. It has support from police reports, newspaper articles and other historical documents. The fact is that many people have died or gone crazy in that building. Nobody since the first family has stayed beyond six days."

"I see. Well, I will read the book and take all that into consideration," I admit.

"You may as well. That copy is free for you," she tells me.

I nod and say goodbye. It is getting late and I need to get home. I suppose I will just have to defy the odds. Anyways it seems no one else had this information.

CHAPTER 5: THIRD NIGHT

Dinner was an excellent repeat. Steak, after all, is always a good meal. I needed it to strengthen my resolve. Over the meal and after, I have been skimming the thick book I picked up. I only need the basics of this house's haunting. Unfortunately, the book states that trouble picks up tonight. But I think I can manage it though. Feeling as ready as I can be, I lie back on the living room couch and close this heavy book.

From the chapter, the tragedy of the Easton family occurred and reoccurs over a six-day period. The Society noted that the seventh day is Sunday and believe the sacred nature of the Sabbath is what limits the loop. I don't know about that, but they have done the most research.

They speculate what transpires each night is because of events that originally took place leading up to the deaths of the family. The Society wrote that the only certain date was 1 May in 1907. On that particular day, the Anglican minister rode out to investigate the Estate after parishioners had realized no one had seen the family since last Sunday. Peering through the windows next to the front door he saw Mrs. Ellen Easton hanged from the railing. The minister fled and brought back the police and a number of curious people who happened to see the distressed minister.

After the group broke down the door to investigate, they found the father shot dead amongst his prized hunts. Mr. William Easton, a former Rough Rider and successful businessman, was found dead in his own trophy room. The Easton's daughter, Elizabeth, died with 13 stab wounds in the conservatory. The trail of blood went from the kitchen, through the living room and she died right in front of the piano. What matters to me is that each night gets more and more intense.

Whispers and murmuring can be heard throughout the house on Monday. I guess thanks to the horror movie marathon, I missed out on that. Ignorance is bliss when there is no real present danger. The second night, the one I fully encountered, has Mr. and Mrs. Easton hash out some fierce argument. When a person checks up on the scene, the two rush out of the room. The Society reports claim that most gave up on this evening. Most that kept their sanity turned tail then. So, I am already tougher than most, I guess. Or stupid. Well, it was weird. It's not like I can give up, my parents plan to live here. I know they won't take any of the haunting business seriously. Not from any secondhand accounts, this book or my own, anyways.

Night three, tonight, is more violent. But like the night before, it is conditional. The ghosts go about their business, but you have to engage them for there to be danger. If you try to climb the stairs during the ticking of the grandfather clock, Mrs. Easton will push you down the stairs. Meanwhile the trophy room will smell of tobacco, opium and gun oil since the room doubled as Mr. Easton's smoking room. If visited on this night, you may get locked in there and have to endure the hazy smoke and his vengeance. I think the reports of opium make what happens there unclear. The Society did not actually go in there during their stay. People in that event reported being in a stupor and seeing terrifying visions.

As for the daughter? She is apparently more withdrawn. Tonight, she sharpens all the knives in the house and then goes to play the piano. Given that nobody in my family has ever sharpened a blade, her efforts will be appreciated in the long run.

Speaking of music, I could unpack some things in the conservatory now. I intend to live here. I'll beat this haunting. Mom and Dad said we can't go back. And anyways, I am not interested in returning to Georgia. Plus, it would be fun to say I overcame the challenges of a haunted mansion and live there. Leaving the living room, I cross the entry over to the conservatory.

The black and white tiled conservatory has heavy stain glass windows that catch the afternoon sun. It paints the room in bright reds, greens and blues. I get the impression that this room was designed to show off the Easton's wealth. Apparently, I read, Elizabeth was a skilled pianist. She learned back east in New York before they came out to this frontier. In this room, the family supposedly entertained guests with her recitals. I am glad I never had so much pressure to play. I'm okay, but not concert good. I was ordered to learn it for the math benefits.

I have a box I can unpack into the built-in bookcases. This room has the fewest things going in it because we've never had a space like this before. In our old house, all the music stuff fit on top of a used piano. Digging out all the music books we own, far less than a single shelf filled and—done.

I take one of the books off the shelf and flip it open to a random page. The house included a piano. Our old one wasn't very good. It probably needed a lot more than just a tuning. In spite of the wear and tear of this house, a piano has been perfectly preserved. I found it under a ton of dusty sheets. The book mentions that this glossy black grand piano was abandoned by one of the later residents in the 80s.

I press the middle C key. The thing is in tune too, or close enough that I can't tell. I learned to play at school on a keyboard and practiced on that old upright. I've never played on a grand. While money was never an issue for my family, we lived cheaply. Mom and Dad always wanted to live out West. Work finally brought my parents here. I don't know the whole story, but it has something to do with low taxes and lower cost of living. Hence, we went from a small house in the suburbs to a mansion in the Dakotas. My life would have taken an absurd enough turn if I didn't include the supernatural.

I start playing. It's a jazz piece in a book full of them. The song fills the room and for a moment, I think I experience history. I can just imagine Elizabeth playing in this very room over a century ago. The Society's book had some pictures of the Eastons. Her father was very sharply dressed in a suit with a perfectly trimmed mustache. He looked old-fashioned and in that past. Her mother in those big dresses looking utterly Victorian and gothic like what I see in the horror movies set back then. She, Elizabeth, always looking well-dressed in what I'd presume is probably the latest fashions of that day and age.

The song flows by and time goes with it. What a view into other lives this room must have had? What did other residents encounter when they moved in? What hopes and dreams did they have? What excitement was felt when trying to settle into this grand old estate? They must have felt terror and madness too as the dangers of this place drove them out. If only walls could talk.

Elizabeth plays this piano almost every night according to the book. She plays haunting, dark tunes it reports. It makes me wonder what songs she entertained her father's visitors with. What did the other following residents play? This is after all, practically the piano room. As I come to a close with the random song I chose, I realize I have had my eyes shut. I reach the finale. I improvised the end of the tune before me. Well, I have never been able to do that before. Looking at my cellphone, I see that I have been playing for much longer than the pages before me. What a captivating piano.

Standing up I stretch. I can feel exhaustion setting in. I can feel the strains of the day. All the biking and reading has left me physically and mentally drained. So tonight, I will crash on the couch in the living room. Down here, I can evade Mrs. Easton's "pushy" behavior completely that way.

✦ ✦ ✦

Music wakes me up, it's the piano. From a glance, I find it is now 12:15. I missed the start of the haunting tonight by 15 or so minutes. Oh well.

Listening closely, this song is familiar. It's not one of the haunting, sad ones I have heard. Rather it is more familiar. It's one of the ones I played earlier! It's an older one—Lennie Tristano's *Yesterdays*. However, she's older than this work. She's better than me at it and that has to be the first she's seen of it! So, does that mean Elizabeth plays whatever music is lying out? I don't recall seeing that mentioned in the Society's research.

Ghosts are supposed to be obsessive, possessive and repetitive according to all the accounts I have read or heard. They often react to human observation, but not in this way! The theory from the book holds that longing and unfulfilled wishes binds them to an area or object. This emotional binding limits their behaviors. Actually, it makes them quite predictable once you get past the supernatural aspects of it. I guess it is a mixture of hellish torture on earth and postmortem OCD. But this, Elizabeth's playing of my songbook, breaks the pattern.

As I try to reason my way through this unexpected behavior, the song ends. Now if she is obsessive, she'll play it again. Another action could be to play her sad song or something else in the book I left out. After a pause, another song begins. It takes me a moment to recognize it. It wasn't in the book I left out. I don't have the whole piece memorized, but our books are by genre. I left a jazz book out, but now this is a classical piece from the 1920s—one of Gershwin's, I think. So, she can pull things off the shelf? So much for patterns and eternal obsessions.

Now this I have to see. Getting up I exit the living room. I should be fine so long as I stay to the lower floor and clear of the stairs. Out in the entry I can smell the mixing of gun oil and tobacco. It seems to come from the trophy room. Mr. Easton is sticking to his pattern at least. I pause in front of the stairs. Looking up them gives me no chill down my spine. I feel no unconscious fear from looking upon them. I guess I haven't provoked Mrs. Easton yet. Good thing the violent ones have a script and stick to it.

Anyways, time to witness something different. I pull out my cellphone as I approach the door. I wonder if I can get a video or picture of this? This could go big. I check the screen. It's blank. I try the power button, no luck. Figures. But I thought I charged it before dinner? This must be some sort of paranormal electronic interference.

Oh well, to eyewitness this will have to be enough for me. I put my cell away and pause before the closed conservatory doors. What will she look like? As I reach for the door handles, something makes me stop. There's something around my neck. Odd. Something rough, it's round and coarse? It's a rope?

I grab at this thing, putting my hands between it and my neck. Then I am yanked backwards! My hands just barely stop the loop from crushing my trachea, but I still fall over! Before I can get up, I am dragged backwards. Towards the stairs! IT's A NOOSE?! HOW!? I kick out, trying to catch myself on something, anything! Meanwhile my hands protect my windpipe from the rope's bite. My flailing bats boxes aside—but nothing stops me!

Some force of unworldly strength pulls me up the stairs like a reeling in a fish. I try to catch a rung on the railing with my foot, but the damn thing snaps, breaking away uselessly on my shoe. Each bounce up the steps hurts. My hands are pulled red raw from holding back this noose.

In my twisting around I manage to see my, my attacker. A ghastly form, Mrs. Easton's translucent body simmers in an old-fashioned dress. She looks at me, her eyes two bloodshot black voids. Unearthly rage projects from her body. I have now reached the top of the stairs. I feel frozen in place.

Reeled in, I am now in her clutches. She has a strong grip I can't seem to break. I see the end of the line lashed securely to the railing. Now, I realize my peril and snap out of my awe. Trying to slip the noose off me, I can't! My hands are caught with my neck in the loop. I won't get strangled quick, but I can't fight back.

Mrs. Easton adjusts her grip. Her transparent hands are not

of this earth. Somehow her ghostly form can touch me. She has a solid grip that is freezing cold and yet somehow it burns too.

I try for a kick. As a lifeguard, they trained me to handle drowning victims trying to stop my breathing. Though nothing prepared me for this! Even the disparate drowner lacks the power of a vengeful specter. Her strength absolutely ignores my twisting efforts to escape her vice grip.

In spite of her small stature, little muscle and mortal bones do not limit her strength. She intends to toss me over. She lifts me over her head. One arm slips out of the loop and I try to hit her, but to no avail. And she releases!

I snap my right arm out and grab a banister as I fall. Her expression grows even more hated. In a rage, she kicks my hand to dislodge it. Pain courses through my fingers. No!

I fall. My reached-out hand grabs at the rope. It combines with my stuck arm to prevent the noose's snap from breaking my neck. As I swing freely, I realize that this is now an endurance match. How can I escape while twisting on the line!? Even if I could, she won't let me live. I can feel her hell-heated hatred stare down at my defiance. If I let go, I will die strangled. Even if I escape, she'll try again. I don't think I can win against her unrelenting murderous intentions. She's too strong and determined. A flailing arm and luck only got me this far. And, I'm not winning.

I hang, time before the inevitable seems to drag on. My arms burn, and my grip slackens. They're getting numb. In this struggle, I somehow twist and look up. I can see her gaze. It is a demented patience. Her spectral form glows in the light of the moon. I feel the weight of my whole body. T...This must be, the end.

A flash of light appears above me. The rope somehow snaps! I find myself weightless! Falling! A knock and a rainbow of colors overwhelm my vision as the world disappears.

CHAPTER 6: ???

I open my eyes. She was trying to hang me! This leaves me gasping. That ropes rough grip, I feel for it. There is nothing now. Just my sore and probably bruised neck. I'm safe?! How?

The entry. I'm here on the first floor. Some boxes must have broken my fall. But, "I'm alive?"

From where I am lying, a gleam of light catches my eye. Buried into a wood panel is a kitchen knife. Picking myself up, I go and investigate. It's one of our steak knives. Using a footstool, I get up high enough to pull the blade out. It takes a bit of work. It's really stuck in there. Somehow by working the blade back and forth, I get it loose and remove it. The blade has been sharpened significantly. Though I am no detective, I can guess that this blade came from the direction of the conservatory. I roughly trace the flight path with my eyes. One of the conservatory doors is open as if to confirm my suspicion.

Why would Elizabeth save me? Putting the knife back in the kitchen, I go and check the book I left in the living room. The Society's text mentions nothing about her intervening. Or at least when I first skimmed it. I guess a closer reading is required. Whatever the case, things are not adding up.

For one thing, Mrs. Easton attacked unprovoked. Her trigger for last night should have occurred when I climbed up the stairs, an action I never did. I technically fell up a flight of stairs at her initiation. They aren't supposed to be this aggressive, well, at least not last night according to the book.

Leaving the house then should be the first priority. I need a different place to stay for tonight. I am smarter than to tempt fate. This is day three—no? I think it is now day four. Night number four is worse even if things stick to the patterns the Society mapped out. I figured I could hold out at least to the fifth night, but if patterns won't hold—I'm out. Plus, I am in no condition to defend myself. I am tired and sore all over.

In checking my cellphone, there's no signal. But it is now 11 AM.

CHAPTER 7: FOURTH DAY

That doesn't add up. It's morning, but it's still dark outside? No light is coming in from the windows. I head out to the back porch. It must be dark because of this fog—a very thick fog. It will be tricky to navigate the twisting dirt road in these conditions. Strange, I can hear rain, it patters on the roof. However, I can't see it out the back of the house.

I go back inside and head over to the front door. Outside the window, I see it is raining over here. What little I can see does tell a lot. I find that the road is muddy to the point that there is no way I am getting out of here with anything less than a jeep.

Trapped. Damn it! Unless this mess clears up, I have no way to get out of here safely. Plus, I have no wilderness survival skills to speak of.

No signal on my cellphone.

I try calling anyways. Sure, there are no ghost-busting groups available. Though, I should be able to get the cops to come pick me up.

Of course, it doesn't work. I'll try again…and again.

I cannot get it to connect. I guess that leaves the landline. It's hooked up, but I am not sure if it works. Though at this point I'll try it anyways.

Heading back inside, I try the telephone located just off the dining room. No dial tone. I try dialing anyways, but no luck.

Of course. By now, I should have expected that.

I clearly can't leave the house and I cannot stay here if foul forces continue to haunt the place. A catch-22, this is in between a rock and a hard place. My situation is utterly clichéd. In spite of all this doom, I can at least acknowledge that irony.

Well if that's the case then I need to solve the mystery of the Eastons. That's normally how you resolve this sort of thing. Damn it! I'd rather watch the film than live the story! There's a flash of light and then in the distance, some thunder sounds. The power goes out. Great, now I can't even watch a movie. So much for escaping physically or mentally.

Well, being that it is daytime still, I can at least wait out the fog. The sun typically burns that up by the afternoon, presuming this state follows a normal weather pattern. Considering how dark it is, I had better locate the box of candles and a flashlight. Mom's fondness for buying scented candles may help. We should have a ton. Granted they smell something awful when all burned together. I think that box was put in the entry...

I have decided that I don't particularly like the entry anymore. Bad things happen there. I know that trend will continue. I can still feel the marks on my neck. The strains of work, evading death and falling—It's wearing me down.

I press on—got to find those lights. It doesn't take long fortunately. I find the candles next to one of the boxes I smashed on the way down. I check those crushed boxes. Lucky, I found the towels when I landed. An undamaged box nearby has a radio sticking out of it. Perfect. I knew I had seen it recently. Maybe I can get a weather report?

I take the box of candles, the radio and a flashlight lying near the door and head for the living room. I am in luck; the radio already has good batteries in it. Turning it on—there's nothing but static. I scan through the channels with the dial and extend the antenna. Nothing on the FM, so next is AM band.

A woman's voice comes over the radio, "Attention, Attention. Delta, Romeo, Lima, Hotel. 9-7-8-1-9-8-0-5-9-2-0-1-3. I repeat: Delta-Romeo-Lima-Hotel. 9, 7—" What is this crap? I turn the device off. So much for a weather report. All in all, I cannot seem to contact or get information from the outside world.

I suppose the last thing to seek is the pistol. I know that I could kick Mrs. Easton and she was tangible enough to toss me. Mom and Dad surprisingly kept one gun at grandpa's insistence. Some story goes with it of when they were a new young couple moving to the big city. They taught me how to use it mainly so I wouldn't do something stupid—I guess like this. But I have no other choice. I have bruises from blows I landed on her. Hopefully lead will have a better result.

The case I locate in the kitchen. The unassuming gun case is hidden in what could probably pass as some briefcase at a glance. The lock code is simple: "1984." I think Grandpa set it. He had certain beliefs. My parents never did tell me about them. Inside I find the weapon, its manual and two magazines of ammunition. I would prefer anyone but myself to handle this situation. But I guess some things I'll just have to do myself. Maybe a gunshot will get people's attention?

The living room becomes my base of operations due to its central location in the house. I can either escape out the front door or slip through the dining room to the kitchen—there's a garden door to the outside too. On the other hand, there is the hall that leads straight out back to the porch. Unfortunately, there are no religious objects amongst our things. Supposedly ghosts are repelled by them. Mom and Dad always considered themselves scientific and rational—I think 'agnostic' is the term.

I was sided with my parents, before. Though these events may have me reconsider that. Now that I think about it, my family's "rational reasoning" was not because we were directly informed. I mean they are office workers, our entire collection of books comprises of eight really heavy cookbooks, five music books, and the rest are books I needed or thought I needed for school. My parents aren't much for reading either—they won't have many more to add to the shelves. Now that I think about it, my reasoning has been based on the assumption that I didn't need to look it up. I always presumed the modern world had already figured everything out and that ghosts and horror were the products of fiction and entertainment. If I survive, I'll need to rethink my beliefs.

Lunchtime. Maybe I can grill something since the power is out. The propane grill is under the porch cover, so it's out of the rain.

*　*　*

It's been a couple of hours, maybe. I'm trying to save battery life with my cellphone turned off. Now it rains in the backyard too. The rain seems to have gotten worse. Also, the fog shows no sign of lifting. I tried reading, but the scented candles bother me just as much as eyestrain. Combined scents had the expected result. Reluctant to take the stairs, I stick to the first floor. On the covered back porch, I just stare out into the fog. It is so dense. You wouldn't guess there's a forest out there.

A sudden gust of wind rushes through the mist. I am presented with a view of the former carriage house that was out back. Only the moss-covered stone foundation remains. The rest, according to the Society, was burned in arson. The story was that some high school kids did it because their friend wandered in the house after his girlfriend dumped him. The police claimed it to be a suicide. The boy was found hanging from the balcony. The enraged high schoolers turned arsonists had intended to torch both structures out of vengeance for the house's curse.

The Society found accounts of the crime diverged. The fire department officially claimed in its report that they stopped the teens from getting the house. So only that building was destroyed. Years later, the Society gathered personal accounts. All interviews of the grown-up high schoolers stated that the carriage house caught flames "with a fury of hell-scorched tongues." Also, personal accounts from both firemen and the former alleged arsonists stated that they teamed up. They claimed to try and burn the buildings under the logic of destroying a cursed place for the greater good of the community. Whatever the case, the house would not ignite. Ultimately, nobody went to court and no charges were pressed. It just seems people moved on and avoided the house as much as possible.

As the fog slowly rolls back in, the ruins disappear in the mist. I think I hear a clock chime from inside. It's a still, eerie scene. Then there's movement. Is that something in the ruins? Is there someone out there?!

The fog is brushed away with a sudden gust of wind. A woman's pale form stands out there in the middle of the ruin. She appears to be looking for something. Growing a little bit clearer, I can see better. It's Mrs. Easton! Her terrible form is unforgettable to me now, engrained in my mind.

What is she doing out there? The fog rolls back in. Her form and the ruins disappear into that mist. There wasn't anything like that mentioned in the record. The carriage house was just the servant's quarters and a place to keep the horses.

This place is driving me crazy. I need to get out of here.

CHAPTER 8: FOURTH NIGHT

I overslept! I was exhausted when I decided to take an after-lunch nap in the living room. Outside is pitch black now, probably and still raining! I guess I am stuck here for the night. I wish I had a car.

It doesn't help that things haven't added up. I have been skimming through the book by candlelight and found that I have encountered things that don't match up with prior accounts. "Ghosts, those souls bound to the mortal plain seem to adhere to particular patterns, maintain certain habits, and usually behave consistently," it claims. Wait, "seem" is in there. I need to read more carefully. Still, I feel like it is cheating to basically claim, "Ghosts are predictable, except when they aren't."

Some parts are consistent. Elizabeth sharpened all the knives. The only constants are the irrelevant parts. Mrs. Easton is aggressive. The Society never claimed that. They stayed in the house for four nights. Is the pattern broken because I have observed it? Is this one of those things, where history is useless?

Rolling over, I fall off the couch. Ow.

No point in getting up, the carpet is comfy enough for this bruised body. The sounds of thunder remind me that I can't just walk out the front door and leave. I look at the entry from my position. I can see a stack of newspapers. Wait. Newspapers? When did that get there? I guess we subscribed. Most news I get comes from the internet. Who knows what has happened since I came out here?

I sit up and check the grandfather clock. It is silent and not working. So I am safe for now. The book says that the clock only ticks at, "the most unholy haunting hours." That's about the only thing consistent about this place.

Nevertheless, I run. Coming out of the living room, I run for the door. Jumping over some boxes, I land next to the papers. Out the window is a world of white. I grab them and retreat back the way I came. The coast seems clear from quick glances. Even still, I feel better back in the living room. I only caught a glance outside, but something white? I find the nearest window and pull back the curtains.

Snow on the windowsill? What is with this absurd weather? Isn't it April? Supernatural weather wasn't mentioned in the book! This state is insane.

I am firmly stuck here then. I can't go out in this weather!

I get it—I'll stay here. Taking out a flashlight, I click it on to read the news. I didn't get today's issue. The paperboy must not have risked the weather. Not much catches my interest. The local news: *The Yellow Sign* does feature mention of the horror movie marathon I watched. They titled it: *Vorwalpurgisnacht-marathon*. I have no clue how to pronounce that. It is a part of something called *Walpurgisnacht*. Apparently, the event is now a mixture of Catholics remembering some person named St. Walpurga and nonreligious celebrations of the spring. Well, those amongst other things are in the article. It sounds like a rather strange event with bonfires and other shenanigans, also there's something about historical witch burning—I'm lost. The article is too complicated to read in this poor light. I'm still groggy too it seems.

There's something about the Easton Estate in yesterday's paper. It's under "Local History." Oh, I overlooked this detail. I guess the Easton's all died on the upcoming vacation. That would mean the anniversary of their deaths is tomorrow.

Not good, are all the patterns different for this week because of that? This book probably then works any other week other than this one. That would explain their habit breaking. The Society wasn't so stupid as to visit the worst week of horror in this house.

I should head out. The woods are probably safer. It's a crazy plan for someone like me. I have no clue what I'm doing out there. Never mind the snow, mud, fog, darkness and lighting—those are natural forces. It's just that the supernatural forces in this cursed house are too much.

So, with madness, I decide to risk going out into the forest. I'm not leaving without being prepared.

Flashlight—check.

Extra battery—check.

1911—check.

Ammo—check.

Cellphone—check. There's no signal, but that could be improved by moving out.

It mustn't be too cold. All I've needed so far is a hoodie when I'm not moving around much. So, I should last the night. Alright, time to go.

The clock chimes.

No, it's too late now! I can't leave!

Wait, all that means is that I can't just walk out the front door. That is just one limitation. There is still the back door. I'll try to take the door to the garden in the kitchen. Mr. and Mrs. Easton seem to not go near that area of the house anyways.

Passing through the dining room, I enter the kitchen. It is dark with only the slight scent of the almost burned out lavender candles I left in here. Flickering shadows cast by the low burning lights and disappear with the temporary flashes of lighting. Creepy. The woods outlined by lighting look even more foreboding. When this is all over, I am going to take some wilderness survival course.

The door to the garden is an ancient, heavy metal door. As I approach, the handle falls off. I try to put the thing back on in hopes that this is a restoration project problem and not a supernatural damnation one.

No use, I can't fix it. I can't exactly take out the door either. It appears to be solid metal. That leaves the back door in the hall or a large window. Unfortunately, most of the big windows are located on the second floor. Backdoor first then.

This door should be unlocked. I used it earlier today. It's closed. So, I try the handle.

It doesn't budge.

So, that leaves the front door...a living room window it is then. I head back through the kitchen and dining room. That route seems safer. I hear rain patter against the roof. Figures—damn weather. Passing the old grandfather clock, I find it still ticks away the haunting hour. I think I see something out in the entryway out of the corner of my eye.

I don't indulge my curiosity to look and check. Then the piano music starts. No matter, I just need to leave.

First, I try to find the window latch. It would be a shame to smash the window and cut myself on the glass. The latch holds—either rusted shut or by supernatural binds.

Oh well, we are remodeling. What's one more thing to fix? I take a side table and strike the window.

Whatever they made the frame from is very durable. The glass cracks easy, but the frame holds.

I repeat.

Still!? What did they do, hide metal bars in the wooden frame?

I batter away at the damn thing. Then I clear away the glass, but the frame holds fast.

Stopping. I need to catch my breath. It looks like the side table will give after another blow. The window frame is much tougher that our modern furniture. I wish Mom and Dad hadn't kept the power tools with them. I guess I might be able to use the cast iron frying pan—

A gun cocks. I recognize that sound thanks to all the movies I've seen. Naturally, my eyes seek the sound's source. It came from the direction of the entry.

No.

Over from the trophy room, Mr. Easton's ghastly form stands. He wears a safari suit on his semi-translucent figure. Armed, he wields some ancient rifle. His eyes are two blank voids. I am paralyzed by his unearthly stare as he raises his rifle. He's going to shoot me!

My knees give, and I collapse as he fires.

Weak knees save me as the shot hits the window with a ringing noise—sparks fly and the bullet pings off the frame. They did reinforce the window with metal! As Mr. Easton ejects that cartridge, I crawl behind the couch for cover.

Reaching cover, I remember that couches aren't bullet-proof. This won't last. I need to fight back and escape in the chaos. That or hold out until the clock stops and the next day arrives. Both options sound hard, if not impossible!

Somehow the ancient grandfather clock ticks on. How does that old thing still work? Damn it! Mr. Easton lets off another shot, forcing me to hide again. The bullet tears through the fabric of the couch showering me with stuffing. The shot must have lodged itself somewhere behind me in the wall.

His aim is terrible! But still, I need to move, the couch won't protect me! I peek back over. He's already ejected the empty case and fires again! I duck and by some luck, he misses.

No, his aim isn't bad. He's taunting me! Well, I have a gun too! I peek over the top of the couch and fire off two rounds. My shots go wide, missing completely. It's no surprise. I've only ever fired in the safety of an indoor range. Just those silhouette targets standing at various distances. They never shot back though!

I look around, he's trying to pin me. He is crossing the entry with a trained movement. Mr. Easton fires another shot—more stuffing rains down on me.

I need to pull back to the kitchen. It has nice, thick metal doors.

I try to move. He fires another shot. Only because of my hesitance, he misses. The floor at my feet takes a bullet sending up splinters.

I force my shaking legs forward. To stall him, I fire a couple more shots in his direction. Nothing hits. However, as he steps forward more into the entry, a noose drops down around his neck! No one other than Mrs. Easton yanks him up! Why is she helping me!? What's going on?!

Whatever. I'll take it! I retreat, leaving the strangling of Mr. Easton to his damned wife.

In the dining room, I use chairs to block the doors, both the one to the hall and the way I just came. If he escapes and maintains some solid form, he could use either door. I barricade with a background sound of gunfire. Mr. Easton is persistent. Being that he's already dead, I don't expect Mrs. Easton to hold back a combat veteran for long.

But why? Why are those two fighting each other? The result benefits no one but me. Whatever, I can figure it out after I escape.

The kitchen is as I left it. I secure its doors. The records have never mentioned the ghosts passing through walls, so I hope that at least holds true. The door is still there, handless and locked. You know, damage-wise, a bullet to this door won't hurt the property. When I get out of here, I am going to shoot the propane tank. An exploding house might get the cops here faster. But first, I need to get out.

I put the gun to the door lock. I've never done this before, but it should work. Like in the movies. I pull the trigger.

The ringing echo of the shot causes me to fall over. A white powder showers me. Flour? The bullet ricocheted around and hit the flour bag, I guess. I can hear the Eastons fight on in the background even as my ears ring. Looking to the door—still secured shut. I just can't seem to escape!

Suddenly I hear metal straining. I look up. The pot hanging rack I'm under hangs precariously. The weight is just too much for 3 of 4 old chains. Before I can move, the chain gives, and it rains pots and pa—.

CHAPTER 9:
FOURTH DAY?

I feel sunlight on my face. Pain. Sore too. These sensations tell me that I am not dead.

I wait. I don't feel quite like moving just yet. My thoughts are a jumble. I feel dried blood over my closed eyelids. Wiping away some of it, I finally open my eyes.

Ceiling. It's tiled so I guess this is the kitchen. Or, I have the floor and ceiling mixed up. Going by the amount of blood and the dull throbbing pain in my head, I presume head injury. I resist the urge to move my neck. If it's a spinal injury, one wrong move could paralyze me. Good to know that the first thing that comes to mind after a loss of consciousness is my first aid training. It stuck.

Above me are the broken chains of the pot hanger. I guess that it broke and dropped some pots and pans. On my chest looks to be the culprit—one bloodied cast-iron skillet. Grabbing a shiny pot fallen nearby I look at myself in the reflection.

Crap, I look awful. My face is bloodied from the cut on my forehead. At least it seems the wound has clotted. I probably had a concussion too.

All of this means ultimately one thing. I survived the fourth night. Seeing that there is light outside, I presume it's the fifth day—the day before Walpurgisnacht. Although the haunting cycle is supposed to run on some six-day cycle, a gut feeling tells me I still have a long way to go.

CHAPTER 10: FIFTH DAY?

Of course, if I am lucky, that pan knocked me out long enough for this to be Sunday. Whatever the case, I need to leave—now. I think the hospital will take me in based on injury of body and not the madness that caused it. If this is the fifth day, then I have no problem spending the night in the hospital's care. I reach into my pocket. By some good fortune, my cellphone is intact. And the screen is blank. It won't turn on. Did the battery die while searching for a signal?

Now where did I put my charger? It hurts to think. The previous owners, while they never stuck around, almost always had remodeling started before they moved in. Fix up the house, get chased out—there's a pattern to this. If I could just beat these ghosts, I'd get a mansion! Sure, the town is different and a bit weird, but I just need to finish high school!

The power may still be out. Oh, I see my charger over there now. I had put it in that box of kitchen appliances by an outlet. Convenient.

Using the kitchen island, I pick myself up. My legs tremble. I feel uncertain about standing, but somehow, I manage to get up. They're just stiff and sore from non-supernatural actions related to box moving and bicycling. I tug the cable out of the tangle and set up the charger in the nearest plug. I'd escape now, but in this condition, I know I wouldn't get very far. I may be somewhat fine on my feet but balancing a bike would be pushing it.

Without really looking, I plug in the charger while checking the room. The kitchen is more or less, as I left it. The doors remain shut, barricaded, and above all secure. Other than the mess of pots from my ricochet incident, it is still mostly an utter mess of half-unpacked things now covered with flour. The damn garden door still solidly holds with no handle.

I look back at my cellphone. It is still a black screen. I press the reset button on the outlet. No effect. This better be a circuit breaker issue. That box should be on the inside of the pantry closet. I am glad it's close and convenient. Our old place had the thing stuck down in the basement.

Using the kitchen island for support again, I head over to the closet. Each step is sturdier than the last, but still I don't feel that great. Plus, I'm tired. Being unconscious doesn't count as rest apparently. Sore from moving, beaten from dodging death and this is mentally wearing too. Dealing with the supernatural is soul draining.

Reaching the box, I do find all the switches tripped. I'd like to presume this was some automatic feature but given these supernatural encounters—now I'd say anything goes. I flip them all. Lights flicker on and I hear my phone beep. That means, that means the cellphone is charging! I'd cheer, but I'm too tired. The best I can manage is a sigh of relief. The phone needs a bit of charge before I can make a call.

What was I thinking? Going alone, I brought a gun to a supernatural fight. Never mind I have never handled the damn weapon without supervision or away from an indoor range before. Since when have bullets been the best weapon against ghosts? It would have had the same result with use of my toy rubber band gun. Well, though I wouldn't be covered in my own blood and flour. Or have probably suffered a concussion.

All my idiocy aside, this situation is ridiculous! Ghosts! I haven't believed in such things since I was maybe seven? They ceased to be a worry along with fear of the monster under my bed. By then, I figured they were all fiction for a good story and that people who believed such things to be superstitious fools.

My gaze wanders and eventually falls upon the knife block. Getting up, I feel much better. Going over to the counter, I inspect the blades. Before they were so dull, Mom would have trouble cutting carrots. I draw out a smaller one. The blade is now sharp enough to cut the packing list next to the block. That ghost Elizabeth, she must have sharpened them. Putting it away, I take a seat back my charging cellphone. Tired, I lay my head down on

How am I even alive at this point? Elizabeth saved me from Mrs. Easton. And Mrs. Easton fought Mr. Easton over trying to kill me. Does that mean Elizabeth will take a stab at me tonight? At this point, I notice that several of the knives are actually missing. It was a full set when I unpacked it. I know that set was full when I took it out. We never seem to lose track of knives in my family.

Shit.

I need to leave.

I'm in the kitchen. *Her* domain. According to the book, Elizabeth has a route from her bedroom on the second floor to the parlor, then next to the conservatory and lastly this kitchen. The kitchen where we keep knives, now with very sharp knives. *Lots* of knives. Mom's solution to dull blades was to buy more, but she never threw any away. Putting the knife away and head back over to the breakfast nook.

I need to leave now. I hope my cellphone is ready to go. I'll call for the para—no, the police. Creatively, this interprets as a home invasion. I need to get out of here before the clock starts. Before making the call, I'll sit down a second. I need a bit of a breather first...

Sitting up, I check my cellphone's clock. Where did the time go!? Outside, it is now dark. I could have sworn it was light out when I came to! The cellphone is fully charged though. I must have fallen asleep at some point! Damn it must have been the concussion. It threw off my sense of time. It is only two minutes to midnight and *that* clock's start! Tonight, it is the night...

CHAPTER 11: WALPURGISNACHT

9…1…1…I dial far too slowly. I can only hope that maybe the clock won't start, the police come and I do escape. It's, it's, it's ringing. Pickup, please pickup!

Then the line goes dead. Despite the barricaded doors and the bullets shot, I can still hear the grandfather clock ring in the midnight hour. It rings for my death. The question now—is how? By the noose, the knife or gun? I can't help but sigh. I am tired. How am I going to get out of this round?

Then the lights flicker out. Maybe now I won't see what will finish me. This darkness melts away by a faint glow, a now familiar one of some spirit. I sigh again. Somebody is cutting to the chase.

"Really? Are you going to just accept this?" a voice asks. I presume it is some corner of my mind clinging naively to hope, the madness before the fall.

I turn to face the pale light source.

Beautiful.

Before me stands Elizabeth in all of her ethereal glory. She wears some sort of prairie dress with an apron, her hair tied back in a braid. She looks almost like she stepped out of a pioneer picture. Except this body is unworldly colorless, semitransparent and enveloped in an unnatural glow. Her eyes are two dark voids staring out in the darkness. A big detail is that she holds the largest of Mom's knives in her left hand—a cleaver.

Her expression is hard to read—not a contorted expression of inhuman rage. Rather it seems almost, I guess, curious? Then she opens her mouth and asks, "Can we talk? You've certainly been the most tenacious resident as of late."

She can talk? More so her voice is human sounding, I expected something more anger and anguish laden. I am at a loss.

"Elizabeth?" is the most I can get out before this incredible encounter.

"Well not the swiftest," she muses with a sigh before saying, "So you know my name." The more I hear her talk, the less earthly she sounds. Her tone, there is something more behind it than what people normally have. Something that feels unnatural. I just can't put my finger on it.

I manage to get a response out, "I've read up on the Estate." Talking is good. That means she isn't going to kill me—yet.

Elizabeth fiddles with her dress apron in an almost shy manner. She asks, "So those two managed to put something together."

"It doesn't cover this week very well," I point out. I am having a conversation with a ghost. It's not something I expected.

"I believe the Society visited during a different part of the year," she answers uncertainly before admitting, "Time is sort of a slippery concept for me now."

No surprise there, but "You know The Investigator's Society of Supernatural Phenomena?"

"Two of them, we had some nice chats. Admittedly I am not sure if they thought they were just dreaming? They were so different from everyone else. Unlike residents, they were researchers—inquisitive, cautious, careful and prepared as much as one could be." she replies.

"I think they stayed four nights," I comment.

"No five, I think? Or maybe it was only four? When they weren't looking, I read some of their research notes. The two disagreed on a ton of things. I can't say I fully understood their work, but I only caught glances anyways. They both concluded that they only survived because of my help. For the publication, they planned to focus more on their research over their own actual experiences," she tells me.

"Why?" I have to ask.

"Some of the conversations we supposedly had weren't real. I remember a number of them, but not all of the ones they recorded. It all kind of mixes together," she answers. She leans on the kitchen island and muses, "There is something about this house that does that. It makes you imagine things. I had the same problem when I was alive. Though I credit that to boredom."

Great, knowing my luck some dolt built this over some place of supernatural phenomena. Noticing the Society's book on the island, she gestures towards it. Before she can ask, I tell her, "Go ahead."

She flips through the text musing at certain pages, "I remember the Bradstons. So that was the 1950s. Oh and they found out why the carriage house is gone! They were still in research when they came here."

"When did you realize you were, well, um, dead?" I ask.

"Around the time of the Bradstons. They brought what was called a 'television.' I recall being distracted by it in the first-floor parlor. They saw me and fled in terror, left it on though. I watched some show. It was about the Wild West. Very inaccurate, I mean it was before my time, but there was no way it was that clean. There was another show, it was really weird, like something from a cheap novel, well a weirder one," she answers.

"So, television changed you?" that is something.

"I watched it until 'the power' was turned off. At that moment, I realized I was dead and apparently, a ghost. I had an existential crisis," she tells me, her voice seems distant. She looks out the window with a sad expression.

I guess the supernatural are suspect to change like the modern world. What a realization. Dead, yet still bound to this world. I never thought of what comes next. I guess this is one result...

"What did you do next?" I have to ask.

"Well, I don't recall much from before the Bradstons. There are bits and pieces of me remembering being in anguish and rage. I must have been terribly anti-social and despondent," she admits with a shudder. Looking back at me she continues, "When the clock starts, I wander around the house. Play piano. If I'm lucky, there's a new resident. They usually bring something fun to mess with. There are always some books to read—this glow means I always have a reading light! Also, I've gotten to play 'video games,' 'watch movies' and 'listen to the radio.'" Each of the technological items she mentions sounds unfamiliar, like me trying to speak Spanish.

She then frowns saying, "Unfortunately, my parents chase off or kill residents before too long. Either Mother and Father are unfazed by all the technology or their rage overwhelms any intellect they may still have. Unfortunately, I can't ask them, I am only conscious during the clock's ticking and they don't acknowledge my existence most of the time."

"This is a lot to take in," I admit. Non-ruthless ghosts, modern technology altering the supernatural, it's a bit much. I did suffer a concussion, so my head already hurts.

She laughs, it's a ringing laugh full of life and warmth, something that completely mismatches her form. "Well you are handling it well. You remind me of the twins and their Society. They could stare horror in the eye and ask questions like this."

"You're not horrifying when you're not in a murderous rage from beyond the grave," I admit before adding, "It's more of a strange beauty—otherworldly."

She laughs at this too, "Ah you flatterer!"

The cocking of a rifle interrupts our conversation. Right, her parents. I had forgotten about them. One out of three befriended is pretty good, but the other two are still out to kill me.

"My parents are always a bit later," she comments. The

sound of gunfire and breaking wood tell me that Mr. Easton is working on the dining room barricade. Not good. I check my cell-phone, still no service. Consistently useless.

"Can I stop them?" I dare to ask.

"I doubt it. The Society tried and to be frank, they were actually prepared," she tells me.

I shrug I'd didn't move here prepared for a fight, "So what about escape?"

"Well, you can evade them. For whatever reason, Mom and Dad compete over killing the residents. It is as you saw last night. And the Society escaped because they took advantage of that distraction," she answers quickly.

"How?" I dare to ask.

"Blasted out the cellar door by shooting out the hinges with a shotgun. Like I said, better equipped," she states as it sounds like the dining room barricade gives way.

"How can I beat those two afterwards?" The only way to the basement is through the hall or the dining room.

"I don't know. Get them exorcised?" she suggests doubt-fully.

"I don't know how to do that," I admit. Plus, I think something like faith/belief are required for it to work. I don't admit that though.

"Now that I think about it, I don't think this house was ever blessed," she muses idly. Well her life isn't the one at risk.

The door to the kitchen rattles. They aren't going to let us ponder future steps here and now.

"I can get you downstairs," Elizabeth states as she gets up. I merely nod, and she grabs my left hand. The hand that takes mine is human shaped, but it lacks a "certainty" of physical form. Further, her grip is not one of human warmth, it chills my arm and it seeps throughout my whole body.

She pulls me into the pantry. It feels like what I imagine

dry ice might feel like. Pushing me over against the closed-circuit breaker panel. She lifts a hidden latch opposite revealing a trap door with a small spiral staircase.

No explanation needed. She lets go and I follow her down and close the door behind us. She follows, hiding the ladder access. Her ghostly form serves perfectly as a light in the darkness.

We are now in what appears to be the wine cellar. Excessively dusty, there are cobwebs everywhere on the empty racks. I shudder, it's cooler down here.

"This should buy us time. Servants only used this passage," she explains as she dusts off her dress, an action perhaps done only out of habit. Dust shouldn't bother a ghost.

"Even if I escape, that won't solve things," I admit.

"True, unless you can convince someone to demolish this cursed place," she admits regretfully.

"I doubt it. Some arsonists tried and failed. I doubt the city will let me use explosives," I reply bitterly as I look around the emptied room, somebody cleared out the racks. I can't drink away my problem or have a toast to my death. Checking my pockets, in the chaos, I have ammunition, but forgot the gun. So, fighting back is not an option either. I look at the Society book in my hands. It is open to the introduction page.

We record these encounters to tell stories, to try to explain the unknown, and perhaps resolve some mysteries.

"That's it!" Elizabeth exclaims from over my shoulder. She was reading the same page. Now that I notice her so close, I can feel the deathly chill that seems to come off her form.

"Wh-what?" I fail to conceal my surprise.

"Solve the mystery. I mean, I don't know why my family died," she explains.

"How would that help?" I ask.

"Ghosts are supposedly bound by burning hatred to particular places or things. Figure out the hatred and maybe you can unbind them?" she doesn't sound so confident when explaining it.

"You don't seem to be burning with undying hatred," I point out the obvious.

"Still more information might lead to a solution," she presses, nevertheless.

"I suppose," I can't deny that as I turn to the pages on the Easton Estate. Looking it over I comment, "The Society suggests that the servants likely played some role, but they've never been mentioned beyond the initial account which states they went missing a bit before your deaths."

"That's the two people unconsidered! Ms. Beaufort the maid and cook, Mr. Armbruster the butler and coachman," Elizabeth states.

"Were they the murderers?" I ask. The book found that many felt that was the case.

In their defense, she tells me, "I don't think so. Ms. Beaufort was rather harmless; a delicate young woman and Mr. Armbruster was loyal. Both were well paid—I saw the family ledger once about a week before I died." Above I can hear a gunshot. Mr. Easton must still be struggling to break through the kitchen door. Or fighting Mrs. Easton.

"Whatever the case, I don't think the mystery is going to be solved tonight," I answer.

"I agree. Mother and Father will search the entire house until all residents are accounted for," she says while thinking. With an idea, she says, "You escape and get help. I can tell you are in no condition to do much more this evening."

I do feel the exhaustion setting in. I was tired and beaten before, but now all these supernatural dealings have drained me further. In reply, I merely nod.

"I don't expect you to come back. I mean given what you've been through...I should thank you. I have gotten bored playing the same piano music all these years," she admits shyly.

Suddenly Elizabeth lunges at me!

Tackling me to the ground in her strange form, I see from the dusty floor that a noose has been lowered down the stairs. "Mother must have known!" Elizabeth cries. My neck was just there!

"Spending a century bound to one place could do that," I suggest as we get up.

The noose drops to the floor. I am way too close to it still! Raising my arms so that the rope can't just coil around my neck, I prepare. I protect my neck, but it hooks on my leg, giving me the slip. The otherworldly coil tugs on me. I grab the rope and tug back, but my strength doesn't match that of that beyond death. The most I can manage is avoiding instant strangulation.

Elizabeth moves to help me, but I am pulled back up the hidden passage and into the kitchen. I flop and flail like a hooked fish on the line with no escape. Some strange force commands this rope to pull me through the kitchen. I bash against cabinets and the fallen pots and pans. It drags me through the battle-battered dining room that Mr. Easton's rifle forced open. I take on new bruises, cuts and splinters from the wreckage here and in the living room. There must be some swelling around my eyes as well. It's getting harder and harder to see straight. Somehow, I maintain consciousness as she drags me out through all this mess.

There almost seems to be a pause at the broken, yet still ticking grandfather clock. In spite of its age, it still counts down to my demise.

Once in the entryway, I can see that Mrs. Easton intends to string me up the way she perished. I try to wrap my legs around some box I battered past, but it doesn't keep me grounded.

A second loop wraps around my neck. Then as if to torment me, Mrs. Easton raises me slowly with a pulley setup. First, she pulls me to my knees, then back up on my feet and higher still.

When I am on my tiptoes twisting about, Mr. Easton enters from the conservatory. He raises his aged rifle and fires not at me, but at his wife!

The rope slackens, putting me back on the ground. This is my opportunity to move. I can't seem to remove the rope, but I can put some distance between us.

I see Elizabeth come up the basement stairs and she throws a knife above me. I can feel the line slacken and the noose seems to melt away in the air. I'm free!

Now to escape! I throw my whole body at the front door!

It doesn't work! My strength is too low, and its lock is bound both by worldly durability and supernatural force. I almost black out from the impact as I recoil back from the immovable door. Nevertheless, I try again. This second strike is even weaker and shoots even more pain throughout my body. This isn't going to work!

I'll try the back door. I turn around and bolt. Bumbling and tumbling over and around the spilled boxes in the entry, I reach the clearer hallway. I abandon the two ghosts fighting. I don't know where Elizabeth is.

With a straight shot at this door and a whole hallway to pick up speed, I charge. I throw my whole weight at the door. I black out a bit as I hit the wood. But I can feel it buckle and wood cracks. The door gives way!

Rolling off the porch, I spill out into mud, pine needles and slushed snow. But I am out and saved!

Somehow, I pick myself up from the ground and run. I've got to get out of here!

How I am able to move is through pure adrenaline. It doesn't make me coordinated though. I trip and land face first into mud and slush. Looking back, I tripped on a rock. Wait, no, a stone brick. This is the foundation to the carriage house! Shit. This is still part of the ghostly domain! I can't keep this up!

Looking around, I see I landed in the midst of the ruins. Lit by the moon, they almost seem to be still smoldering. This may be a part of the house, but there is little that can hold me within.

No walls, windows or doors remain to stop me!

I look back, that was a mistake. There on the back porch, Mr. and Mrs. Easton seemed to have set aside their eternal conflict to see to my death. I can see a rope lashed to a support pillar. Following its path, it leads right to a loop still on my foot. As if because I noticed it, the line tightens, digging in around my ankle and once more they tow me back. This time the couple is pulling me back, hand over hand.

Once again, I am failing around as they reel me back to a certain doom. I try to stop. I lock my knees and try to brace myself against some of the ruined foundation. This crumbles away, and I unwillingly come closer to the house.

Through mud and pine needles, they drag me closer to my death. I grab a pine sapling, but it snaps with a coordinated tug from the two of them. I release the broken tree and try to grab anything else. Soon though, too soon, they have brought me to the foot of the stairs.

Elizabeth appears through the smashed door. In all her spectral glory, she wields a cleaver in one hand and a large chef knife in the other. With twin blows, she hits both her parents with a blade each. She puts a knife to the back for Mr. Easton and a cut to the head for Mrs. Easton. Her blows knock the two down.

Standing over their fallen forms, she realizes what she has done. "Mother... Father," Elizabeth struck her parents. Horror in the face of the immortal is a deeper expression than that of anyone alive.

Mr. and Mrs. Easton however are undeterred, only delayed. Rising up, the blades stuck in their bloodless frames, they lash out with vengeance against their rebellious daughter. Mr. Easton strikes with the butt of his rifle and Mrs. Easton lands a few blows with her heel. They strike without speaking, without a sound beyond the blows themselves. Elizabeth lets out inhuman screams of anguish of trauma, betrayal and a pain that transcends the physical beating. She knows what she has done and its price.

I try to loosen the line cutting into my ankle. It is too tight from being tugged through the forest! Meanwhile, the parents batter Elizabeth to the ground. From her apron, my gun falls. I grab it. And with an ease I haven't ever pulled off before, I reload from the ammunition I still have on me.

With a new magazine, I aim. Practically point blank, I can't miss. I owe her something for saving my life so many times.

The first shot hits Mr. Easton and the other Mrs. Easton. I alternate firing at the two. My shots catch them off guard and they are forced to cease their offensive against their own daughter. Though I am certain bullets have no lasting damage, it seems that the impact does have some sort of knock back effect.

Elizabeth seeing my help draws out another knife from her apron and from her awkward position hacks me free of the rope. Once cut from the pillar, the line around my ankle dissolves.

She cries out, "Run! Escape! Don't come back!"

I get up again. And I reply, "Thank you Elizabeth!" In a flash our eyes meet, hers two infinite orbs, though inhuman now, I recognize the lonely sadness that deepens their depths.

Freed, I run. Though my strength is near finished, I can feel one last spurt. I run around the house and get on the driveway. I plow through mud and mush melted snow. Lungs burning, each breath I take is a heaving struggle. But I'm free! I'm going to escape! I'll get the Society. I'll figure out some way to bring peace to that house. No matter what, no matter how, no matter when. I will succeed. For her!

I am near the first turn. With this, I will no longer be able to see the house! I can do this!

A single gunshot rings out.

Pain, pain at a new level, it courses through my body like lighting. I can't seem to get my legs to work anymore and I trip. My chest feels opened and I fall into the dirt road. Damn! Deadeye.

With the last effort of the heavy body, I turn to look back. He's there on the front porch. Mr. Easton rises from a kneeling position with war-disciplined ease. He ejects the spent cartridge as the clock chimes the late hour. My body grows lighter and—

CHAPTER 12: FIRST NIGHT

I snap awake with a start. What, where, when, huh?! What-what's going on?! It takes a second to get my bearings. My heart still races from some half-remembered dream. And, it's gone. An old movie plays in the background. It's a horror flick. Right, I was watching the horror movie marathon. I'm on the couch. So, I must have dozed off. Weird dreams triggered by the surround sound, I guess.

I, Henry Torrington, made a dumb decision. I should have just gone to bed.

The situation: after a hard day's work, those moving boxes don't move themselves, I decided to watch some TV in the new house. Correction: the only "new" aspect of this place is the boxes I lugged around and my arrival. The "new home" my parents picked out is at least a century old and does nothing to mask that aging rot. How did the realtor describe it? Right, he claimed, "…run-down—a fixer-upper." Liar. "A drafty ruin" is a better description.

Whatever. After hours of moving boxes, I am sore, tired, strained, and exhausted. Sleep should come easy in this condition. But no, I decided some television would help me relax. Plus, I needed the reward. That and I went through all the trouble to get the cables hooked up right—so many tangles. A cruel twist of fate almost wasted my efforts—the service provider hasn't come through. That means no cable or dish—whatever Mom and Dad picked, or internet yet. I am basically cut off from the outside world. It barely leaves just the local freebie channels. I should have seen that coming. Well, no point in dwelling on the dumb decision to watch a horror movie marathon alone at night in the middle of the woods in an ancient house. I don't care for the next film in the marathon. Why repeat it unless you have no choice?

Time for bed. All that's left to do is navigate one creepy and uncanny horror house in near total darkness. Climbing the creaking basement stairs, the old clock chimes in the living room. I don't feel too surprised. If anything, I get a weird sense of déjà vu. Yawning, I must be too tired to be anything more than disoriented. Just imagining things. It's all from being tired and home alone. My mind thinks old house probably equals haunted. Well, I guess this will make life in the Easton Estate interesting...

CHAPTER 13: SECOND DAY

Sore, I feel it now. Yesterday's strain is today's soreness. I am sprawled out. At least made it to my bed for the night. Opening my eyes, I find myself staring up at the cracked white plaster ceiling. Huh, déjà vu? This feels familiar despite this being an unfamiliar ceiling and box-filled room. It doesn't feel new though—hmm, strange. It should.

This curiosity passes though, and hunger settles in its place. As I take out my cellphone, the only working clock right now, I imagine it is close to one pm. And I'm right. So, I am due for a late lunch.

My cellphone says I have a voicemail. Checking my missed call, I see it's from Mom. She called this morning at 10. Given all that's happened, no wonder I missed the call. Listening to it, I hear they are checking up on me. I already called when I first arrived at the house. Both of them are busy this week wrapping up work. It's why I'm here early and they are still down in Georgia. Still I call back and leave a message that says I'm fine right now.

Getting up, I head for the shower. I know for a fact that I don't have anything left to eat here. A gut feeling tells me to not disturb the fridge. So, the plan: shower, bike to town, coffee, food and grocery store. I try to shake off my sleepiness and actually wake up. I still feel tired and heavy even after a night's rest.

* * *

While I was showering, I had a thought, like a recollection

of something important. Or maybe it was something strange I noticed? But those thoughts slip away and escaped like water down the drain.

As I now pedal down the dirt road, my mind wanders. If memory serves me right—yup. There's the cemetery. The fading gravestones stand in the shade of pine trees. Even in daylight it has a foreboding look.

I am struck by a certain familiarity as I note that the cemetery's barbwire points in all directions. It is an odd sense of déjà vu. It could be a recollection of riding up in the moving truck. The movers picked me up at the Rapid City's airport and took me the last leg up to the house. The cemetery would have been the first thing I saw of this new hometown. Now that's a dark realization.

That trip was an experience. After my first airplane ride, I got off and saw endless miles of prairie. The drive up took me through my first trip into the hills. Harris, one of the movers, apparently knew a thing or two about the area. He gave me a very basic outline of the history out here. I don't recall the whole thing, but the cemetery must have come up.

Passing the Memorial Chapel, I conclude they must have a lot to remember here going by the number of statues and monuments out front.

Finally getting into town, I can fix this hunger and caffeine shortage. I locate a place called *Kaffeehaus Neu Welt*. That should handle both issues. It has a coffeeshop look. Locking up my bike out front, I head inside.

Crowded, apparently this is the place to be for a late lunch. Booths and tables are busy, and the bar seating is full too. Now what?

Someone near the back seems to wave at me, signaling for me to come over. Obeying, I find a guy about my age in a school uniform with a blue blazer writing a letter.

He says as I arrive, "You can sit here."

"Thanks," I reply and take the seat across from him. I can't help but offer the comment, "Busy place."

"This is the place to be at this hour. People need coffee to carry the afternoon," he muses while raising his own mostly emptied mug.

Before we can exchange another word, a waitress comes up to our table. In a black dress with a white apron, she appears to have stepped out of another era. "Can I take your order sir?" she asks. She even sounds like she came from a prior age.

As I take the menu she recommends, "In no offense sir, you look like you need a cup of the red eye. The extra caffeine looks to be your main interest," she is an angel.

"Yes, I'll take that."

"Right away sir," she then departs.

I take a look at the menu. They mostly do breakfast, coffee and desserts. Oh, the lunch offer is a Reuben. I do like those.

Satisfied that I know what I want, I set the menu down. I look to my table host. He seems to be wrapping up a letter with a signature. His handwriting is an elaborate cursive I can't read upside down.

As he folds the paper he explains, "A letter for my pen pal." He sticks it in an addressed air mail envelope and seals it.

As he finishes, I tell him, "My family just moved into the old Easton Estate."

"That old place," he trails off as if caught up in some memory.

"It is a fix up project, a big one," I continue.

The waitress returns with my coffee and a glass of water. I take this time to order and she departs again. Then I take a sip of my coffee. There's the jolt I missed. Ah, I needed that!

"Rough night?" he asks, though it sounds more like a statement. He is perceptive like the waitress. Though I wasn't trying to hide it.

"I was up late. After moving some boxes, I got caught up in the horror film marathon. It was a first day with a whirlwind of boxes," I reply.

A clock chimes somewhere as he comments, "Well, I have a few more classes to attend and I don't want to lose off-school grounds privileges."

"Oh of course. Goodbye," I bid him as he quickly packs up.

"Yes, until later," he replies.

My anticipated Reuben is here, and I intend to enjoy it at this time.

Post lunch, I decide to visit the bookstore. I believe it is on the way to the grocery store anyways. *Lorraine and Daughters Book Emporium* appears to be *the bookstore* to visit in this town. The massive place probably is a reader's paradise. I'm not one for such, but something draws me here.

The interior is a maze. Overwhelmed, I randomly wander down an aisle. Books fill the shelves that tower over me. I think there's book stacked on top of them too.

Seeing a bay window ahead, I head towards it. Coming to the end of the aisle, the space opens up some with a sign overhead reading, *The Local Pens*. Around the window is a seating area with a desk and comfy looking chairs. The shelves facing the reading area must be devoted to local authors then. I guess I could learn about the new town. After living in suburbia, I guess living in a place with history could be different. Most of the books are on mining, cowboys, outlaws or Native Americans. Makes sense, I am out West now.

Scanning the shelves, one book in particular catches my eye. It's an oddly foreboding book. The title reads: *The Paranormal, Supernatural, and Cryptozoological Report on the Black Hills*. Pulling the book off the shelf, its cover bears the seal of a group called the *Investigator's Society of Supernatural Phenomena*. It has a motto too: "To seek that which dwells just beyond the mundane world." It also has a sticker that indicates that this is the store's copy.

Somehow, for some reason the look of this book catches my interest. I open it and take a seat on the bay window bench that looks out on a quiet cobblestone side street. Comfortably settled in, I dive in:

About the Authors: The Investigator's Society of Supernatural Phenomena (ISSP) operates as a club at Columbia High School in Eur-

opa, South Dakota. Ten teens conducted exhaustive research to discover these things unknown or forgotten to modern humanity. Their findings may challenge conventional and normal perceptions of life, history, and nature.

They sound a bit dramatic, like adventurers of old or in video games. A black-and-white photograph depicts the ten in clothing befitting of 19th century explorers in what appears to be a hunting trophy room. One of them looks familiar. He might be the boy I met at lunch. Now there's an interesting development.

Am I supposed to take this seriously? The book is no lightweight read. The topics cover the range of bizarre and paranormal: weird animals, lost caverns, elven kings, haunted mines, cosmic horrors, etc. It all appears to be a bit ridiculous, but they wrote on several topics. The chapters even feature notes at the bottoms of the pages.

Oh, there's a section on the Easton Estate—my new home. I ought to get this book. Mom and Dad might get a kick out of this chapter. Looking back on the shelf, I see there are no other copies over there.

I guess I'll have to go request a copy at the register—wherever that is. The title is easy enough to remember, so I return the book to the shelf. Diving back into the forest of books, I hope I can find my way out.

Luckily, the signs have a path through the maze. Soon, the front desk is dead ahead. An older woman, reading a worn hardcover book, staffs it. Looking up, she sees and greets me saying, "Good afternoon young sir. What can we do for you?"

I tell her, "I need a copy of *The Paranormal, Supernatural, and Cryptozoological Report on the Black Hills* ma'am."

"It's currently sold out," she says before checking the computer. She adds, "And on back order. That one is a hit with tourists and locals find it amusing. Plus, it looks great on the shelf with that 'old world look.'"

"How soon are more due in?" I ask. For some reason, I feel a sense of urgency. I grip a railing under the counter tightly.

"I can take down your name and address and we should have more in after *Walpurgisnacht*," she answers.

A gut feeling tells me that then it would be too late. Even though I don't know when or what she's talking about. I push down that doomed feeling and reply, "That's fine. I'm Henry Torrington." Digging out an envelope, the address is weird, and I haven't memorized it yet. Finding it, I add, "I live at Easton Estate —"

"Wait. You're the new resident up there!?" I am cut off. She looks at me in a new light—a worried one.

"Yes," I reply—it's a grand house, I bet it will be the talk of the town.

She then crosses herself and tells me, "God have mercy on your soul. At the Society's request, we hold a reserve copy for the new residents of that cursed place." She then produces a copy of the book from under the counter.

Handing it to me, I find it is a signed copy from all the members and has a message. It reads in a fancy cursive, *Free to the inhabitants of the Easton Estate. May Time be ever at your side.*

"I will be sure to read this," I reply to the clerk. I think I recognize the handwriting as coming from the letter that guy was writing. It's easier to read right-side up.

"It's a good book," her tone is, I guess, reserved. The Easton Estate part seems to have cooled her reaction to my interest in the book.

I thank her and buy a tasseled bookmark with something called a jackalope on it to show that I am not just skimming the shelves. With the current time, I might as well just get some fast food and head home. It is later, and I don't feel like going to the grocery store on my bike.

CHAPTER 14: SECOND NIGHT

This book is utterly captivating. I started reading it while eating dinner. Normally, I am not much for reading books. I'll read for school, but that's for the grades. This book, however, is actually interesting. Maybe because I now live in the supposedly haunted house that it's about. I have a vested interest.

So, according to this, the Easton Estate is essentially one of the most haunted places out West. In spite of that infamous history, it is almost entirely ignored. I think though that has to do with the location. I had to look up this state before explaining and re-explaining where I was moving. Apparently, most people thought I was off to Canada.

Anyways, the story for this house is ridiculous. Death and madness swallow the many residents that followed the original owners: the Eastons. There's a lot in here. I read the research on this house through dinner, while doing dishes and managed to make my way into the living room on the couch. A lot has happened here. There's quite a bit to read through on it.

I finally manage to pull myself away from the book when I reach the end of the section on the house. There's a lot more to this book. Maybe, I'll take a look at the fairy tale one next? My cellphone shows the time to be almost midnight. According to this, that ancient grandfather clock will soon start again.

Drained, I literally read for hours. I relax, settling deeper into the couch. The contents of the Society's research were horrifying and gruesome in extensive detail. Then they put in footnotes, referring things like newspaper articles and police reports.

I'm just not used to reading this type of thing. I had to reread a lot of it just to follow their process, which was to state simply: methodical.

The clock starts ticking and strikes midnight. My blood runs cold. Night two is not dangerous according to the book, but it is strange. Upstairs, the Easton parents argue through the night. They only interact with mortals who disturb them. Knowing that, I'll avoid the room. Even if this is all superstition, that's up at the top of the stairs. I don't want to fall down a flight of them!

I hear them! Muffled, but there are raised, angry sounding voices. It sounds as if they're arguing. It's coming from somewhere else in the house. If I hadn't read up on things before, I'd bet I would just assume it was a radio left on. I just cannot make out what they are saying though. To distract myself, I look back at the book and recheck the clock section. Even though I read the whole part on the house, it is quite a bit to take in on the first read.

So, for whatever reason, the old grandfather clock only starts up at night. It always ticks when something ghostly occurs. The Society thought the clock had something to do with the haunting. But, perhaps ironically, lacked the time to investigate the possibility. It doesn't look like they could figure much out from this clock. I can only imagine the complicated gears in the thing, I know I wouldn't know where to begin. They figured out so much.

Some time passes. Tired, I can relax at least. This place, the living room, should be safe.
Piano music then sounds from the conservatory. It is a slow and somber tune. I couldn't have heard it before, but it feels so familiar.

The music gets louder. Soon the song thankfully overwhelms the arguing upstairs. I prefer a haunted piano to unworldly things arguing elsewhere in the house. Although it is a slow and tragic song. The tune is comforting and calming for me as I lay on the couch. Its player is clearly very skilled.

❋ ❋ ❋

A chime from the grandfather clock! I am not sure if I dozed off or just stared blankly at an illustration of the clock in the book for over an hour! I must have zoned out while listening to the piano music. It's now 1:30 AM. The second night has passed uneventfully.

I find my eyes filled with tears. There is an overwhelming sense of sadness. It was like somebody was telling me something. Or maybe it's a dream built off of the reading. The contents of the book, the circumstances of this house's history—it's all weighing on me. I guess in some way, I am now a part of this story. This house has stood through tragedy, terror and unending horror. Ultimately, I don't know what part I will play in it.

I stare up at the ceiling and trace the cracks up there. What will my chapter be like? I'm exhausted. That's too much to consider right now. I can't help but realize I am but a mortal in this long enduring house. Time passes, people come and go, but history remains.

Now, I don't want to go upstairs. I don't hear the clock anymore. I'll spend the night down here. Curling up on the couch, I settle in. Tomorrow, I think I will unpack the music room.

CHAPTER 15: THIRD DAY

To start the day, I awoke early and worked on the conservatory. The room is now completely unpacked. Well, there was not much required to do it. We've never had a room completely dedicated to music. It is a start.

Resting on a short break, I lay on a recently uncovered couch. Not original but abandoned by some fairly recent resident. I wonder if Mom and Dad will try and make the house match the original? This couch wouldn't stay. It's that weird modern Nordic look—probably IKEA or a knock off. Though it is comfy at least.

The conservatory reminds me of an odd dream. Or maybe my imagination combines things with what I'm reading. I don't typically remember my dreams. Anyways, the room seems familiar.

My cellphone shows my nap ran long. Well, it is not like I have any appointments to keep. As long as I am working on getting things set up, when I sleep is unimportant.

I get up. For whatever reason, I have a craving for diner food —burger, fries, maybe a milkshake too. I bet there's something in town that can help.

* * *

I almost instantly found the Carsen's Café. It perfectly fits that classic American theme. Parking my bike out front, I head inside. To my surprise I see the guy I saw the other day at the coffee shop. Today he is seated with a girl. Going by looks, they are probably related, maybe even twins.

Walking over to them, I say, "Hello! Small town isn't it?"

"It is, it is. Care to join us?" he offers.

"I will," I accept and take a seat across from them.

"I heard you picked up the book the other day," he comments.

I only need a quick glance at the menu. You order burgers at a burger joint, period. Answering him, I reply "Yes, it caught my attention. Plus, it was free."

"Laura, one of Lorraine's daughters, called me yesterday about it," she states.

"I take it you two were involved in the publication?" I ask. I already know, they're very recognizable and match the picture inside.

"Yes, we were members of the Society before it was disbanded," she answers.

"I don't think I introduced myself the other day," he states.

"No, now that I think about it, you didn't," I realize this too.

"My brother has never been one for introductions. I am Cassandra Scipio, and this is my brother Danna," Cassandra finally introduces them.

"And I am Henry Torrington," I reply before commenting, "Danna sounds like a girl's name."

"That's why I don't like introductions," he replies with a sigh. Before I can apologize, he continues, "Don't worry about it, it is traditionally."

"Most refer to us as the Scipione twins. Names aren't that important," Cassandra muses.

Remembering the original line of this conversation, I ask, "So which part of the book did you two write?"

"We researched and survived the Easton Estate," Danna admits.

"Excellent, do you have any ideas on how to overcome the haunting part?" if they know, then they should help me. I am afraid the stakes are higher than anything else I have ever done.

"Well our records show we got out before it got too ugly," Cassandra admits, "Most of the stuff on being in the house that went in the book was from my writing. There's still a lot of the mystery unsolved." She huffs in frustration and adds, "Our research is also on hold given the forced disbandment of the Society."

"I put in the history part, but my firsthand account was a bit muddled," Danna confesses. Cassandra looks annoyed with him. They exchange some glares. I'm guessing they didn't see eye to eye when writing.

A waiter comes over and takes my order for a burger, fries and a coke. When he leaves, I decide to break up this sibling fight.

"Well, can you two help me survive?" I ask. I feel like I need any help I can get.

"Probably," he states.

"I mean we almost made it a week," she adds. Neither of them sounds very confident.

"Well, to be honest, we weren't planning to stay past a week," Danna admits.

I ask, "What happens after week one? I'm hoping to fix this issue before my parents arrive."

"Nobody's lasted that long. Never more than 5- or 6-days tops. As far as interviews might indicate, the whole haunting mess just restarts," Cassandra repeats basically what the book speculates.

Our food arrives, it looks like we all ordered the same thing. Hunger takes over and we eat in silence. This burger is superb. Beef must be better closer to the open range.

Getting to the fries, I ask again, "Well the book was good, but is there any chance you two might be able to help me yourselves?"

The twins share a look that I can't read. Then Danna answers, "Well today is Tue—"

"No, it's Wednesday," she corrects him.

"Right," he glares at her as he describes, "It's the eve of the fourth night for all the dangerous parts. He then pauses unexpectedly. There seems to be an "aha" moment of some realization. "But you already know that."

"Cut to the chase," Cassandra interrupts him, "The problem is that we are technically forbidden from visiting the Easton Estate. The Society's shenanigans are infamous, and your realtor has the Police Chief on his side."

"Figures," I muse before taking another sip of coke.

"We got a stern warning when the house was sold," he adds.

"Cops are scary," I agree. However, "I am certain the place is haunted. The evidence suggests something kills or drives everyone who lives there mad. Your research proves that! So, why do I have to take the fall!" I end slamming my hands on the table.

My raised voice gets everyone's attention. I pause, it occurs to me that we're in public. Oops.

"Well we know that. People don't let the bad history stop them—the school board, police department and realtor made that clear," Cassandra points out in an angry whisper.

Danna appears angry too. He says nothing as he gazes out the window.

I take a breath and state, "Well then, I just need to win." They both nod in agreement at that. Having their attention, I pitch an idea, "Now in the movies ghosts always have something binding their soul to the earth. Could this just be a matter of solving the mystery?"

"It's untested, but they were brutally murdered. That creates resentment more than most cases," Cassandra hesitantly agrees.

"We've tried, but still, nobody has solved their murders conclusively yet," Danna adds.

"So that makes my idea a possible solution," I state.

"Yes. Our main success was pulling together a lot of evidence and mapping out their predictable patterns each night," Danna says and after a pause adds, "We've got the groundwork done at least."

"The key must be the servants," Cassandra concludes, "No

solution confirms their whereabouts beyond 'they disappeared.'"

Danna checks a pocket watch and states, "Perhaps we should put a pin in this and change locations."

He has a point, too many eyes are watching us. Given the Society's infamy, we might attract the police.

I need these two to help me, "Agreed."

"Right," he says as he writes something down on a clean napkin and leaves it. Getting up, Danna states, "Well, we have some errands to tend to. Our cousin should be home later this week."

"Yes, of course," I reply, "Goodbye."

Once they leave, I grab the napkin. It reads:

Meet us at the bookstore at 3:30 pm. Ask to see
"Gemini." Also, destroy this message.

Cool, I feel like a spy! I use the napkin to wipe up some ketchup and then stick it on my empty plate. I have 30 or so minutes to wait. I then spot a waiter carrying a tray of milkshakes for the corner booth. I think I know how to pass the time.

About halfway through my chocolate milkshake, a police officer enters the diner and approaches my table. I'm a bit busy enjoying the rich flavor.

He addresses me saying, "Afternoon sir. I do hope those Scipio twins aren't causing you any trouble."

"Oh, none at all," I reply. I don't really want to talk to police. I know I haven't done anything wrong, but concern is still there.

"Mind if I talk to you for a minute?" he asks.

"I don't mind," I lie.

He takes a seat on the bench the two formerly occupied and says, "I had heard they were here."

"Yes," that's something I cannot lie about.

"You had lunch with them," he states.

"That was circumstance. I happened to join them," this particular meeting wasn't pre-arranged.

"Well, the Chief wants me to remind you that their work is fiction," he states. His badge reads Officer Harry Orthendrop.

"The house is a bit creepy, good for a ghost story I suppose," I state, I don't feel like arguing will help me at all.

"Glad you understand. If those two give you any trouble call us," he says getting up.

"Oh of course," I agree so as to encourage him to leave.

He seems satisfied and bids me goodbye. Once the door closes, I check my cellphone. I should have time to finish this milkshake, visit the restroom, and head over to those who can actually help.

✳ ✳ ✳

Returning to the bookstore, I find a woman at the desk. She's younger than the clerk from yesterday, so I am guessing she is one of the "daughters."

I ask her the coded phrase, "Can I see Gemini?"

"Follow the signs to the planetarium," is her only answer. She doesn't even look up from her eBook.

"Right, thanks," I tell her before heading in deeper to the store. Signs point the way to the planetarium.

Reaching a large elevator, I see in its directory that it's at the top floor. I guess that explains the dome on the roof. Pressing the up button, the door opens to reveal a big elevator with a couch and a side table filled with books. Interesting.

Reaching the top, I walk down a short hall to reach the entrance. Inside is exactly what I saw when I was in elementary school. Well this one is smaller. The planetarium has chairs angled upwards looking at a projection of the night sky on a domed ceiling.

I easily spot the Scipio twins who are seated looking up. The rest of the room is empty.

Cassandra notices me, elbows Danna who appears to be sleeping, and says, "This location draws less attention."

"I agree," as I take a seat next to her, I mention, "Officer Orthendrop visited me over a milkshake."

"We got out in good time this time then. He's not one for superstitions. He's typically the chief's runner for this sort of thing," Danna comments sounding pained.

"He seemed annoyed, are you two prone to hijinks?" I ask, they seem like they'd be causing all sorts of trouble like on TV shows.

"Our misadventures would make for some great stories, maybe books," the two admit in stereo.

I comment at that, "Well, let's add one where I live and can join in on future antics."

"Right we can try at it. Well, while you were running interference with the cops, we did some more thinking," Danna states.

"Yes, our notes indicate that Mr. and Mrs. Easton pose the biggest threats," she cuts him off.

"Yeah, I know," I don't need them telling me again.

"Of course, their daughter seems to be neutral or may possibly side with me," I state as I find the one constellation I do know. There it is, the Big Dipper.

"At the very least she's not a threat," she agrees.

"How did y'all escape the house the last night you two stayed?" I ask, the book left out the details.

There's a pause, I look over and can somewhat see in the dark that they are clearly conflicted on what to answer.

"We suppressed that particular detail in the publication of the book. The police think we had someone on the outside bail us out," Cassandra finally states.

"If people found out the Society was armed, well, we wouldn't be having this conversation," Danna adds before finally admitting, "But we used a shotgun to blast off the hinges to the cellar doors."

"Hmm. I'll keep that in mind. The house needs remodeling anyways," I reply. No wonder the Society got shut down, they sounded even crazier than reported. Teens with firearms. I guess the stories of the Wild West do have some truth. Though my classmates back home were wrong, they do have indoor plumbing out here in "the sticks."

"What else was left out of the book?" I ask.

"Well, the house seems to jumble memories and messes with the imagination," Danna says.

"Like?" I ask, this sounds interesting.

"You might think you went through some event, like the fourth night. But then, you'd wake up or snap out of some trance and realize that it was only Tuesday," Cassandra states.

"Strange, I have been having some weird dreams," I tell them.

"Well we left the dream part out because my brother's and my journals conflict on the events that transpired in them. Though mine were more accurate," Cassandra says.

"How much do you remember?" Danna asks ignoring her barb.

"Not much, I should have written things down," I realize now how amateur I must be compared to them.

"Well, you should try that. Though don't be like my brother, he took notes on the computer and they were all messed up. I think the supernatural screwed with his technology," Cassandra says as she elbows him.

"Right," Danna says distantly, he seems to have not noticed.

"Anyways, play things by the book and you'll make it pretty far," Cassandra concludes.

"Yes, but isn't their death, um, anniversary coming up?" I ask.

"True, they were probably murdered on Walpurgisnacht," Danna muses.

"That's supposedly a day as haunted as Halloween," Cassandra explains.

"Some gut feeling tells me that detail makes it all the worse," I say, my lunch feels a bit unsettled by that thought.

After a pause to consider that problem, Cassandra suddenly states with confidence, "I think we have three venues for solving this problem in the house."

"Do tell," Danna replies with a tired sigh.

She explains, "One—solve the mystery. Figure out why they died and who did it. Knowing that should free their worldly bonds. Or two—survive Walpurgisnacht, that would overcome the ultimate challenge and possibly defeat them. Method three is call for a priest. What's your preference?"

"Not religious, science has more proofs," I admit.

"Really? Ghosts are a fringe pseudoscience at most," Cassandra says.

"Family hasn't been too taken by it. None of us prefer the 'fire and brimstone' preaching. I might reconsider if I survive this ordeal though," I tell them.

"Hmm, well without faith—divine intervention is less likely," Cassandra states, "Plus, someone already tried that in the house."

"So that leaves us with two options," Danna concludes, "Solve the mystery and overcome their attempts at murder and madness."

"Well, I have the patterns. So, let's work on the mystery," I state.

"Right, well we need to figure out what happened to the servants. They completely disappear from the records and they aren't ghosts to our knowledge," Danna points out.

"Well how far did you two get before you were forced to publish and disband?" I ask, "We might as well pick up there."

"We need to investigate the ruins of the carriage house. That's where the servants lived. There in the second story. So, it will be tricky—there's not much left to work with," Danna states.

"Alright," I agree.

It gets quiet. I find myself staring off into the false void of space. I don't think we can do anything else here.

"Perhaps we should exchange contact information," Cassandra suggests.

"Sure," I agree and pull out my cellphone.

They pull out their own phones. Cassandra has a sleek modern one and Danna has a small, very old looking one. Switching mine to contact mode, I hold it closer to theirs. Cassandra's pops up first and then Danna's too. I am surprised that old clunker can do that.

Now, I have to ask about their names as I fill in the contact notes, "Where does the last name Scipio come from?"

"Well, we aren't of Italian or well Roman descent. Grandpa claimed it when he got off the boat at Ellis Island. It's not really his last name, but he filed the paperwork and it stuck. He also then died with the secret as to why," Danna answers.

"Not much else to say about that," she dismisses the story before stating, "Now anyways, if things get ugly, you call the cops first."

"Of course. I figure if things go that way, I'd claim there's an armed burgl
ar," I tell them.

"Smart move. They probably wouldn't take a haunting seriously," Danna states before concluding, "Good. Then we'll go home and comb through our unpublished notes and see if there's anything we're missing that we should already know."

"I'll try to survive another night and look around the house," I say before asking, "Who should I call first?"

"Me," Danna answers, "My phone picks up signals better. Call even if you think you cannot connect."

"Why is that?" I ask.

"Because that house is confusing, don't assume or give in because your disoriented," Danna replies. He then draws out his pocket watch and checks it again. And adds, "Now if you'll excuse me, I think I am expecting a call from our cousin Antonia."

"Of course, see you later," I say has he gets up and leaves. It's dark so I can't read his exact expression, but he sounded anxious.

"Right," Cassandra sounds confused by Danna's statement. She then says to me, "My brother is weird—well in your eyes we're probably both weird."

"Ghost hunters and real ghosts—normal is long gone," I reply, though, "What about school?"

"My brother and I normally have near perfect attendance, but we're both playing hooky today for some reason. He insisted.

If you think he's weird, I think he's more so today," she confesses.

"Why are you following him then?" I ask.

"He's got something brewing and I know he'd be there for me if I needed it. Our family motto is *'Family is Foundation'* after all," she says before adding, "Well, I better get going as well. Now if I were you, I would wait about five minutes and then leave out the front. Depending on how bored the cops are today, you might be under surveillance."

"That's creepy," I tell her.

"Well, the Society really pissed them off. Goodbye!" she bids me.

"Of course, goodbye," I reply as she leaves.

Left alone in the planetarium, I can't help but wonder at the changes my life has undergone. Never would I imagine that my entire life would change by moving into the middle of nowhere. Ghosts, an odd town, adventure seeking twins, mystery and danger! I've stepped out of my mundane suburban life and into one of fiction. It almost feels clichéd like a movie.

CHAPTER 16: THIRD NIGHT

There is something about tonight that makes me feel uneasy. My throat feels tight and I just don't like the entryway. I get goosebumps every time I even go near there. I can't overcome this growing worry. The clock should be starting soon according to the book.

I got some groceries after the meeting with the Scipio twins. Getting home, I discovered that something had been left forgotten in the fridge on the move up. Whatever it may have been, it has now molded into something else unrecognizable. In hindsight, I had a bad feeling about something from the move. I about damn near lost my lunch on tonight's dinner. Fortunately, I didn't, and we have a mini fridge. I'll need gloves and a gas mask to take on the big fridge's contents. At least it has a good seal. That disaster is contained for now.

I put on the stereo while I cooked and ate. After meeting with the twins, I realized how alone I really am out here. I didn't have any particularly close friends back in my old place—a group I hung out with, but not a memorable bunch. I cannot say I missed them personally, but I think I miss the company. Out here is just wilderness. I have talked to less than ten people and maybe seen less than fifty since my arrival. This new location just feels empty.

After dinner I looked around the moss-covered foundation of what used to be, well, practically the garage. The old carriage house is now just a ruined stone foundation. Charred rock outlines its place, so it's nothing. I had no clue what I was doing poking around there and gave up as soon as it got too dark to see. Maybe an archeologist can read more about it. I can't make anything of it.

Now lounged in the beanbag chair, I check my phone again. It's almost time. However, this evening I am holed up in what used to be the library. It's very large, but not empty. Our unsorted boxes and furniture got put here. Most of this stuff has been inherited and in storage until this move. I don't look forward to sorting through it all. Though, if it weren't for this, the house would be rather empty.

Bored, I decide to call Danna. Listening to music can only pass so much time.

It takes a couple rings, but he answers, "Hallo, ah Henry, everything alright?" he asks.

"No issues yet. I figured I would check up on your end of the investigation," I tell him.

"Nothing major of note, my sister and I reached an impasse on these matters a while back. Were you able to check out the remains of the carriage house?"

"I did, it isn't worth note though. I don't know what I am looking for in the old charred remains of a foundation," I report.

"I guessed that, we'd probably need an expert to learn anything," Danna replies sounding just as annoyed.

"Well, what did you find, anything remotely useful?" I ask.

I think I hear some clacks on a keyboard before he answers, "Well, Cassandra found nothing of note in her records and went to bed. I'm still working through mine."

"And?"

"Mr. Easton can seek a person anywhere in the house and Mrs. Easton's rope—well—by some accounts it searches the house and tries to strangle residents. It sounds kind of like a snake. I don't know if that is true though. Panic tends to make people exaggerate," he tells me.

I ask, "Good to know, which night?"

"Fifth, by most accounts. But the noose can function like a booby trap as well. The accounts are a bit vague on how that works. I guess just be careful of your surroundings?" he sounds a bit confused.

"Alright," I answer. Oh, I wonder, "How is your cousin?"

"It seems she dodged the bullet this time. She should be back for Walpurgisnacht," he answers quickly.

"What is this Wal-purge-thing I keep hearing about?"

"Well, this town is a bit more European than your typical American town," he starts.

"Yes, I have noticed it is a bit different," I leave out 'weird' to be polite and because it isn't the strangest part of my move up here.

"Well, it is the saint's holiday for Saint Walpurga, but most of the town likes to celebrate the Central European holiday six months the opposite of Halloween. There are some darker occult aspects for some, but most use it as an excuse to have a bonfire, dance, eat and drink if you're old enough," he explains.

"So, an excuse to party?" I surmise.

"Preserving cultural heritage guarantees it as a regular occurrence," he agrees.

"Point for tradition. I think I might like this town. What do you do to celebrate?"

"With my cousin in town, we'll go to Mass for the feast of Saint Walpurga. Then we'll be downtown for a bonfire. It will all wrap up in time to finish before the haunting hour. If you'd like, you can join us at the bonfire before handling your haunting problem," he offers.

I accept, "I'll join you, that sounds fun,"

"Great, wear dark colors. The bonfire starts at sundown. But I recommend getting downtown earlier, there are some really good food stalls—it's a festival."

"Sounds great!" I tell him.

Then the clock strikes midnight. Its chime can only mean one thing! Quickly I check the signal—no bars.

"Danna! Danna!" I yell into the phone.

"Heard you. Ow, bit loud there. Now was that the clock?" he replies.

"Yes, but my cellphone says I have no signal. I state while triple checking it again. The thing shouldn't work!

"Hmm, odd," Danna doesn't seem surprised. I hear a few more clacks on a keyboard, I guess he's taking notes.

"Well," I calm down with a deep breath. I am fine, "I'm holed up in the library, so there shouldn't be any issues," I tell him.

"Should be a good move, don't get curious and wander out into the entry or trophy room," he reminds me.

"Of course, no worries there. I'm read up. I know better than to do that," I assure him.

"Good, you're smarter than most protagonists in a horror film. Even smarter if you stick to that word," Danna comments. He is absolutely right on both counts.

Getting up, I walk around the room. As I move about inspecting the empty shelves, I comment, "Any chance this house has any secrets you missed?" A quick run of my finger along a shelf finds a thick layer of dust.

"Likely, we don't have original blueprints, so I suppose the house could have a secret passage or room potentially," he speculates. I sneeze at trying to get the dust off my finger. He adds, "Gesundheit."

"Dusty," I comment.

"It is old, each new resident adds a few things, but nobody's stuck around, Most never reached the 'dusting phase' of the move in," he comments.

"That explains the modern stuff like electricity and plumbing," I agree as I take a seat on the bay window bench. It creaks very loudly.

"What was that?" Danna asks, he must have heard it easily.

"The bay window bench, I'm sitting on it. It will need a cushion," I explain.

Then I hear the piano, "Elizabeth is playing now," I tell him.

"I can hear her, she typically plays one of two songs," he comments, "This one is different."

"She apparently will try music left out," I tell him. I feel cool for discovering something new.

"She's curious about new stuff in the house, but I didn't know that," he admits, sounding impressed. He types some more on his loud keyboard.

There's suddenly a cracking noise beneath me! I jump up to see that the bench broke, cracked down the middle.

"What was that?!" he calls.

"A built-in bench, it's by the window. It broke. Apparently couldn't handle my weight," I comment as I look at it, "The whole house is run down, wait."

"What is it?"

"I think I see something through the crack," I tell Danna as I move a broken piece with my free hand. It snaps off with ease. "The bench is hollow."

"Like secret compartment hollow?" he asks.

"No, like," I grab a flashlight and shine it down. Oh, wow.

"No like..." he urges.

"Like a secret passage," I reply, "There's a ladder here." A bolted in metal ladder leads down into the darkness.

"Curious," he replies.

That curiosity is very tempting to chase. I have the sudden urge to climb down the old ladder and explore. Then I hear Elizabeth start on another jazz piece. Common sense hits and I tell Danna, "I'll check it out when it isn't the haunting hour."

"Probably for the best. This is completely new information," he agrees. Keys clack furiously on his end.

"Well, you'll need to get out here and update your floorplan," I tell him. I'd rather not explore this alone anyways.

"Cassandra would be on board. Though the police know my family's cars. The soonest we could slip up there would be on Walpurgisnacht when the cops are distracted with the festivities," Danna states with disappointment.

"You two have a jeep—can't y'all just off-road up here or something?" I point out.

"Depends if there is some sort of trail or logging road nearby. Let me check," he tells me. Then I hear some rustling of what is probably a map. He's actually going to map it out.

While he plots a course, I back away from the window. I don't want to accidently fall in or be sucked in—given the supernatural hour. Safely on the other side of the room, I check my cellphone. The battery is draining faster than I'd like. I think it's because of the spotty service. No, it says it has no service, then how is this call working?

"I've got a route," Danna states, "Well maybe."

"Maybe?"

"Well the usual constants apply," he tells me.

"Like?" what is he talking about?

"I haven't taken this particular route before. I don't know the road conditions. Oh, and weather of course."

"Why? What's the weather forecast? Are we expecting snow in late April?" I suggest the ridiculous.

"South Dakota's unpredictable weather is always a constant," he admits.

"Alright," I have my doubts, but he's a local. "Well, try and drop by tomorrow. I need to get off the line and recharge my cellphone."

"Alright," he answers, "I'll try to get over tomorrow, want me to bring anything?"

"Some cokes, I couldn't fit any on my bike," I tell him. I really need my own car.

"Will do, see you later," he wishes me.

"Alright, goodbye," I then hang up.

It's a gut feeling, but—yes, I figured as much. The outlet here in the library either doesn't work or it's out due to supernatural forces.

The music then stops. Elizabeth must have finished the piece. Danna and Cassandra wrote that she periodically wanders around. Although perhaps against some survival instinct, I do want to meet her. There is no record of her being evil and murderous. Mostly the records note her curiosity, knife sharpening, and piano playing. I don't get the knife part though.

All of a sudden, I notice the door to the hallway is open. I distinctly recall leaving that closed. Damn classic haunted house!

Or did she do that?

I peer out of the library and go into the hallway. It is almost silent except for my breathing and the clock's ticking in the living room. Only pale light floods in from the skylights. I guess the moon and stars are brighter out here. I don't need my flashlight with its fresh batteries. I'll save it for later. I bought a whole package of batteries at the store. Too many movies have a dead character from a dead flashlight.

If the piano is silent, my guess is that she is in the kitchen. She mainly tends to wander between the two according to the book. Although I'm not stupid though to believe that all the patterns remain consistent. Danna and Cassandra both admitted they didn't have all the answers. They only gave the record of what they experienced in less than a week and a history compiled from raving mad survivors. Who knows what remains unrecorded? What was lost either to the limits of research, madness or death?

The hallway has doors to the kitchen, dining room and trophy room. All those doors are shut thankfully. From the direction of the trophy room, I can smell the mixing of gun oil and smoke. Mr. Easton was a renowned hunter—a white man's man in that era—a military officer, businessman, rich and strong. He may also have been a member of some secret society or white supremacist group. So, not really someone I'd like or get along with. He lived an active life is the most certain detail.

I should be fine, he only attacks those who try and bother him at this hour on this night. With the closed door, there should be no problem. I can rest with ease. I retreat back to the library.

In the hall, there's a loud crack! I poke my head out again—not good! The trophy room door was flung open! That's not supposed to happen. No, no, no, no! He's supposed to be closed up in there tonight!

I turn head and rush to get out on the back porch. I don't need to stick around and see what happens next. I practically slam into the door and try its handle. Shit—it's locked! I fiddle with the knob and try again. The worn gears may not always catch. Still locked!

I turn around and see the ghostly form of Mr. Easton come into the hallway. His semitransparent body wears an old-fashioned military uniform. More concerning is that he carries an old rifle.

Noticing me with his void like eyes, he raises his gun. Some unknown instinct makes me dive to the side. I lunge towards the only opening—the now open door to the kitchen.

Behind me is an ear-splitting explosion as he fires. I can feel splinters from the door rain on my back. Somehow, I wasn't hit.

I ignore the lesser pain of landing on the kitchen tile and get back up. I need to find the case. It should be in here. Come on, come on, come on! Where are you? There!

I grab the gun case and put in the code: 1-9-8-4. It worked, good! I pull out a pistol and two magazines. I cannot stop shaking, but somehow, I manage to load it.

Somehow over the ringing of my ears, I hear the sound of his footsteps and ejecting of the spent casing clatters to the ground. Quickly, I turn around and slam the kitchen door shut so hard that I am surprised it didn't snap in half.

The footsteps seem to stop near the door! The old floorboards cease to creak. Knowing that a wooden door isn't bulletproof or even locked, I move away. I take cover behind the kitchen island.

I need to get out of here! Bullets won't work against a ghost! Mr. Easton slowly turns the doorknob, it squeaks with rust and age. This is torture!

I try the metal garden door, but it's rusted shut.

I hear the door to the kitchen rattle. Looking back, I see that somehow a chair barricades the door! Its back wedged against the knob. I don't question it. Elizabeth must have helped me!

"Thank you!" I call to my unworldly helper. There is no response from her, I don't even see her. However, Mr. Easton's reply is to begin striking the door.

I'll slip out through the dining room. From there, I'll cut

through the hallway and retreat back to the library. I think I can break out through the bay window. I cannot flee out the front door, Mrs. Easton will get me. If Mr. Easton isn't sticking to the written routines, who's to say Mrs. Easton won't do the same?

Going through to the dining room, I close that door and barricade it with another chair. My luck is that the ghost cannot apparently pass through solid objects!

At that thought, I hear the kitchen door give way. He's way too aggressive. That just means I need to leave. Why fight and die when I can escape and live!

Out of the dining room, I tiptoe down the hall. Since he's started on the next door, I should have some time. Caution will keep me alive.

A noose lies on the floor before the library door! That has got to be a trap! Mrs. Easton must have figured out my escape route! Also, the door to the library is closed, I distinctly remember leaving that open.

I'm not stupid, I cannot go around the trap. She'd expect that. I know there's usually a second trap on the alternative route. Instead, I grab a large umbrella propped up against the wall in the hall. Thankfully nothing has been put away, so I have plenty of random objects to work with.

I put the umbrella in the noose and then give it a tug. The noose tightens, and the umbrella is ripped out of my hand. It zips down the hall towards the entry. This house is a death trap! I have to get out of here!

Trying the library door, I find it locked. Impossible! I know I left it open and I don't think there's even a lock for it! The book did mention that doors randomly open and close in addition to locking. However, this is all too inconvenient to be random!

The dining room door cracks under the beatings from Mr. Easton. I'm running out of time! I guess I'll try the back door again. Mrs. Easton clearly is still holding the entry as her base.

Another loud crack from the dining room urges me on. I try the back door again. It's locked, Mr. Easton's bullets didn't punch through the door, so I doubt my pistol will break it.

I have no choice. I have to try the entry.

As I head towards it, I notice the basement stairs. Of course! I forgot! I'll escape the same way the Scipione twins did! I rush down those rickety old steps, hitting the light switch on the way. Somehow, that light actually works, and I can see the cellar doors sit on the side of the house. I rush over and try to push up on those heavy wooden doors to open them. Of course, they don't budge!

I hope a pistol can handle the hinges! I fire a shot into one of them. The bullet warps the metal enough for me to rip out a couple screws with my bare hands. I cut myself in the process. The loud shot leaves my ears ringing as I fire at another, repeating the process.

Somehow again through my ringing ears, I hear a creak of a boot on the top of the stairs. I need to hurry!

I rip out the screws of the second warped hinge and one of the doors gives way! I dodge aside it as it falls down. Then I lunge outside.

Outside! I run. Not far, tripping, I tumble to the ground. Needles and pinecones break my fall painfully.

Scrambling low and close to the ground, I find cover behind a large rock. Leaning my back against, I feel my heart racing. It takes me a moment to catch my breath and the ringing lessens.

I did it! I did it! I got out of the house! I'd cheer, but that's too much, I am exhausted. Looking out, I find a dark forest. It's lit only by the stars. Where am I going to go now?

Daring, I peer over the rock. At the basement door, I can see Mr. Easton's ghost. His spectral form seems to notice it is being watched.

He spotted me! Raising his rifle, he's going to shoot!

I duck and my head hits someth—

CHAPTER 17: ???

I think I hear a siren. It's far away. It's cold. I feel rain drops. I open my eyes. White mist is everywhere. My head dully throbs. I'm soaked and it's raining. What's going on?

CHAPTER 18: FOURTH DAY?

"Good afternoon," a voice near me says.

"Amend that—morning is the more appropriate description given his condition," her voice is familiar.

It's the Scipio Twins! Wait? What?

I sit up quickly, my head throbbing. I'm lying next to a large rock in the mud. Feeling my head, I find a bandage up there.

"What happened?" I ask. Opening my eyes, I find Danna standing before me in a mud drenched tan safari suit with a brown, wide brimmed scout hat.

"Well," he looks over to the house and then back to me, "You came out of the basement door and in a rush bonked your head. By the looks of things, I guess you shot out the hinges with the gun you have there."

I look over, kneeling next to me is Cassandra dressed similarly in a mud drenched safari suit, though she wears medical gloves and sports a cowboy hat. Those gloves are covered in dried blood. That is my blood probably.

Seeing that I noticed her, she asks, "Now how many fingers am I holding up?"

"Four," I tell her.

"Good. You hit your head hard, but these sorts of injuries are always bloody," she states as she carefully removes her gloves.

"How did you—oh," I just noticed their old, mud-soaked canvas topped jeep.

"We got through the backroads this time. Apparently, the main road washed out," he explains.

"Our radio picked up the police. They attempted to drive up here last night, but they got stuck on the way up, got out and then gave up," she explains before ordering, "Don't get up yet."

"I thought I heard sirens at one point," I admit.

"Probably them then," Danna agrees as he hands me a coarse wool blanket.

"Somehow you didn't die from exposure, hypothermia or head trauma," Cassandra comments failing to hide her surprise. She then adds, "Though I hope you've got a tetanus shot. There was rust on those doors."

"Mr. Easton gave chase this time," I explain.

"Huh," they both say in stereo.

"So, I probably need an ER visit," I suggest.

"First aid does only go so far," she agrees. She then adds, "But road conditions are risky. One jostle and your head wound might prove fatal. I cannot fully diagnose your injury. You could have spinal injuries as well." I was afraid she'd say that.

"As you might see, our trip up wasn't exactly a Sunday drive. Our cousin, Antonia, given her driving skills could probably get us through every time, but's she can't ever be here right now. We might not make the round trip," Danna adds. I'd nod in agreement, but that seems like a bad idea.

At a loss, I just sit here. Danna brings a water bottle and I take some small sips from it. My throat feels better, though my throbbing head is distracting.

This is a nightmare. At least I'm with some rational people. I can see why the twins survived and so many others didn't. Leaning against the rock I struck my head against, I can feel the weight of everything—the house, the haunting, the injuries—it's all becoming too much to bear.

Danna meanwhile unfolds a map and starts studying it. He suggests, "Medical air evac, um, we might need him airlifted out?"

Cassandra meanwhile gets up and heads over to the jeep and clicks on a radio while grabbing the handset. As she fiddles with the dial she says, "With what clearing for them to land? Well, I'll get road conditions."

I feel exhausted. So, I close my eyes.

* * *

Reopening them gives me a jump! I look around—empty bookshelves, piles of boxes and things everywhere...I'm back in the library! I must have dozed off? What was that then? That was some vivid dream?!

Checking my cellphone, now it's the morning of the fourth day I've been here. Oh, and now the battery's dead. Now I can't check my call history.

I must have dozed off in this beanbag last night. Well, the past few nights and days have been exhausting. What a dream! My stomach grumbles—breakfast time.

I should have gotten bacon and eggs. Cereal is boring. Pouring it into a bowl and adding milk, I then take a seat in a chair. The little breakfast nook is convenient.

I guessed I dreamed that I called Danna Scipio last night. My mind is just a jumble of things. I guess no internet and alone are all finally getting to me. That doesn't even factor in the haunted part!

Outside is foggy—very dense fog. I bet road conditions are bad. I guess I won't be going into town today. Something tells me I should be more worried.

With my cellphone plugged in, I give Danna a call. Giving it breakfast time to charge up, it should be fine if I stay plugged in.

"Oh hello, how are you holding up?" he asks upon picking up.

"Pretty well aside from the weather," I tell him.

"The roads are pretty bad, that seems to be a constant," he reports.

"This fog is something else," I agree, who thought weather could be such an interesting topic?

Recalling my dream, I tell him, "Just a second." Leaving my cellphone with him on the line and charging, I return to the library. In there I go over to the bay window. Fiddling with the bench seat, I manage to get it open. It's like my dream! There is a secret passage!

Running back to the phone, I tell Danna, "I think I found a secret area in the library!"

"Huh, interesting," he doesn't sound too surprised. He then adds with a sigh, "I'd like to check it out this time, but the roads are wretched right now."

"Well, you'll have to try and get up here sometime soon," I state. I look out the window, there's a lot of mud. I add, "I think you'll have better luck than my bike."

"Well, I might be able to help you with your cabin fever. My cousin Antonia fancies herself an off-roader. Where we see impassable slop, she sees a path. She'll be in later. It took some convincing, but she's returning early. We could pick you up for the Walpurgisnacht festivities tomorrow," he offers.

"That would be nice. Will the roads have improved?"

"Not according to my sources, but my cousin would prefer this situation."

"Well, I'll be careful with tonight and see you guys tomorrow," I tell him.

"Sounds good, be careful in there," he bids me before we hang up.

With breakfast finished and dishes done, I dig out the gun case in the kitchen. For good measure, I want the pistol ready. I doubt it will be any good against ghosts, but I might need it for a distraction.

A chill of déjà vu runs through me. This place must be getting to me. Ghosts, a haunted house, extended alone time—it's all getting to me. Lots of loud music might help. I might as well unpack some more things. Despite Mom's and Dad's chaotic packing, I think I have figured out their mislabeled system. This has been a series of trial and error. And like everything else, it is mostly error.

I'd check out the hidden room in the library, but a gut feeling tells me to wait to explore it with someone. Who knows what's down there? Also, I don't want to get injured or trapped without backup.

But then again, I am bored, and I need to solve the mystery to stop the haunting. It might be nice to be on the offensive for once. This whole thing is tiring. Moving in was a lot to begin with. Brushing with death and waiting for the dangers ahead are draining. I'd like to solve things before Walpurgisnacht. Instinct tells me I shouldn't wait.

Fixing up my gun holster, I then check the batteries and backup batteries for my flashlight. I think I am ready. Time to head down into the unknown.

Thankfully, the metal ladder rungs are sturdy. Though, I bet if it was during the haunting hours, they'd break. Climbing down, it doesn't go very far underground. This must be on the same level as the basement.

I turn on my flashlight. I'm glad I brought an LED one, it's bright with great battery life. The room is filled with furniture under sheets. I guess this is a storage room? Though how? None of this would fit down the passage I came down in. The room is about the size of the library above it, I think.

With some flair, I pull off one of the cloth covers. I am attacked by layers of dust that leaves me hacking! My nose filled with the smell of stale mothballs. Not going to do that again.

Recovering from the dust attack, I find I uncovered a pool table! Sweet! This is a great find. Now I have to solve the mystery, we have cool stuff in this house. I love pool.

Moving through the room, I find all kinds of furniture: chairs, benches, desks, tables and more. Granted nothing is as cool as the pool table and equipment for it, but still antique furniture is probably a good haul.

The last thing I uncover is a massive bookshelf. It towers over me. The shelves are protected with glass windowed doors. There are a ton of old books here. Like a huge leather-bound bible, some novels and a lot of stuff probably in French by the looks of it.

One book catches my eye. There's no writing on its spine. Sitting on a shelf at eye level, it looks different from the rest. It's tied shut with an old blue silk ribbon. I want to look at that one first.

I try the handle on the shelf and the door opens with a rusted screech. Taking out the book, I try to be careful. I hope it doesn't crumble in my hands. Undoing the cord, I open it. It's not a book. I think it's a notebook or journal, maybe a diary of some sort. Inside are handwritten pages. Unfortunately, it is an old cursive font, something I'm not familiar with. I think, going by the inside cover, it's Elizabeth's journal of some sort. I think I can make out her name. Deciding to try and read it, I take a seat in a rocking chair I just uncovered.

As I turn through the pages, I gradually start to decipher the unfamiliar font. It is likely a diary. It lists entries with dates and locations. Starting in New York and going down to Atlanta—my hometown! And then she goes down to Mobile. There's a number of places in between, but I don't know all of them. She even lands in New Orleans before going upriver to get up to South Dakota. Elizabeth Easton is well traveled compared to me!

Her last entry lists the house as her location, about six months before their deaths. Although it's a struggle, I think I can read the whole last entry:

> *I close this diary on the eve of my new life here in Europa, South Dakota. The house is the finest in the area. None can rival it. Seeing the town—it is full of European immigrants, well-to-do folk who have already done a lot to bring civilization out to the wilderness. I imagine our new home will become the center of society here. I cannot wait to write about that in my next journal. For now, I will place this diary in the secret storage room. Our travels have allowed us to pick up more than our home can show at one time. Hidden behind this bookshelf is a passage to the carriage house.*

This might mean the carriage house is more than a charred ruin! There's a basement to that too? If so, then that means the Scipio Twins missed that! This might be a breakthrough! And I found it!

Looking down, I see on the floor that the bookshelf is set on a metal track. There's a handle on the bookshelf not for any of its doors, I give that a pull. Nothing moves at first, but then it gives way to an awful screech. Metal against metal, my ears ring with its scraping. But I get the secret door open just enough to reveal a stone passageway.

This cannot have been too secret though. This tunnel is too big! It could easily fit any of the furniture I saw in storage. A lot of workers must have been needed to build an underground passage this long and big. I guess they kept quiet and that detail was lost to time?

Venturing inside, I find that this tunnel is dark and dank. I guess some water leaked in? The room prior must be sealed off pretty well. The tunnel isn't too long, soon I reach a pair of wooden doors.

I try to open them and to my surprise they open with little resistance. Inside is a cavernous like room. In the middle appears to be some sort of elevator device. Though I doubt it works now. There's also a heavily rot-damaged staircase that winds up towards what appears to be a trap door.

However, my curiosity evaporates. It is cold down here and I am not dressed for more exploration. This place is very dark, dank, molding and cold. Also, the drip of water doesn't help.

I return the way I came and close the shelf and trap door behind me. Checking my recharged cellphone, I find that it took more time than I expected. It's getting late and I need to eat and prepare for tonight. Given the fog and rain, I'm stuck here for the approaching evening of haunting.

CHAPTER 19: FOURTH NIGHT

It started raining and the power went out. In another call over to the Danna Scipio, he said that his cousin made it home and would be up to bailing me out in the morning. So, I just have to last the night.

Now that is a terrifying prospect. Murderous ghosts for a night. The Society's book is not very helpful for actually overcoming the ghosts. Though to be fair, they did not succeed in solving the mystery. They just did not die or go insane.

Meanwhile to pass the time, I read the diary I brought up from the hidden room. It's an interesting read. There might be something to it. I get the impression that Mr. and Mrs. Easton might have been at odds. I mean they spent years apart for no clear reason beyond the fact that the father sought adventure.

I look out the window. White flakes float down from the sky. It looks chilly out there. Wait. Is that snow?! I pull out my cellphone and dial for Danna Scipio. Calling him is easiest. For whatever reason, calls to him have excellent reception no matter what it seems.

"Yes," Danna answers.

"Why is it snowing?"

"This is odd for this time of year, but not unprecedented right now," he admits.

"Well more importantly will you guys be able to make it?"

"Yes," he replies quickly before explaining, "My cousin Antonia is excited."

"The roads will be utter frozen slop," I state the obvious.

People just don't go out in this kind of condition!

"This isn't the South. Snow and ice are minor concerns," Danna comes back boredly.

"Al—alright," I don't want to deter them. I need them out here more than they need to get out. Shifting topics, I ask, "Did I tell you that I found Elizabeth's diary from before she came to the estate?"

After a pause he concludes, "No I don't think so at this time. Have you had much time to look at it?"

I reply, "I've looked through it. There might be something to it, but we'll have to combine it with everything else you've found out. At the very least it sets up how she and her mother wound up here."

"Well that is a missing puzzle piece," Danna states, I can tell he's curious.

"Also, the secret room connects to the basement of the carriage house," I add.

"Now that's another interesting detail you've come upon. Is there much to see down there?" he asks.

"I think the secret storeroom will tell us more. The tunnel and carriage house basement are molding ruins. I am actually not sure how safe it is to be mucking around down there," I tell him.

"Well, we will bring some masks and gloves tomorrow," Danna decides.

"It also smelled unpleasant," I add.

"Like rotting flesh?" he suggests.

"I don't know that smell. I didn't look around much anyway though," I really hope I don't ever learn that one.

"Just as well, who knows what molds claim that hole a home," he states.

"Well, I'm calling it a night," I tell him, "I'll see y'all tomorrow," I punctuate my goodbye with a yawn.

"Of course," he replies, "Until tomorrow then."

I hang up and look around the library. We've gotten a lot of stuff. Well, I can sort that out later. Now I need to prepare for tonight.

Flashlight—check.

Extra batteries—check. I know how batteries work. If you have spares, they never seem to die. Pistol—check. I doubt it will have much effect, but if available, it might be of use.

I also dig out a sweatshirt and poncho. If I need to leave, I ought to be ready as I can be.

To pass the night, I decide to go back through Elizabeth's diary. In a quick skim she journeys from New York down to Charleston. Then Atlanta and through various plantations in the South before winding up in New Orleans. Steamboats up the Mississippi and Missouri Rivers and a train out of some place called Pierre get her ultimately here. Also inside, she included illustrations to help fill the diary. This is a fun way to record a life's journey. I wish I had this talent.

NEW YORK CITY | November 18, 1905

Father writes that he has bought some land out West. Mother and I are to set off soon. Since the land is undeveloped, we will be taking a roundabout way there visiting Father's and Mother's friends along the way. Finally! A world beyond New York! We are not traveling together; Father will meet us there. Mother and I will be traveling alone. Somehow, I get the impression she prefers it that way.

I cannot really relate to the story. Much of this diary depicts the life of a white, high society girl. Though she has a bit of an adventurous streak. She slips out to explore each place in more detail and meet people. Her sketches show a stark contrast between the two alien worlds. One of high society versus the other of more ordinary life. What a life she lived in such a short time!

I reach a good stopping point. It's when she is about to leave Charleston. I will have to read her account later. It must be really late now. Her diary is captivating. Though, it shouldn't be. It's slow paced—her life is one utterly lacking any sort of action and never gets beyond idle chatter. Still, somehow it is a peek into worlds I have never really thought anything of. It's different and refreshing, I guess?

I suppose I want to get to know Elizabeth Easton now. She seemed like a decent person back then as well as a friendly ghost these days. It makes me wonder though. Ghosts are typically bound to earth by tragedy or anger. I would guess tragedy, but I am curious to know the details. What binds her to this crumbling estate for all eternity?

I stand up and stretch, working out the stiffness of sitting. I feel like I have sat for too long there. Looking up, I try to stretch my neck too. I conclude aloud, breaking the silence, "I wonder what happened to her?"

"Who is she?" someone asks.

Wait what!? I practically jump out of my skin.

Looking back down I find Elizabeth right in front of me! How could I have missed that!

"You scared me!"

"I am a ghost," Elizabeth explains. Her eyes, though two blank voids, somehow seem friendly. Dressed in a dress of a past century, she has a historic beauty mixed in with a pale, ethereal glow.

Calming down my racing heart, I reply, "Of course, that's true."

"Well who were you talking about?" she asks again.

"Oh right, I was referring to you. I found a diary of yours from before you came to the Estate," I answer holding the journal out to her.

"Excellent, I thought I had lost that!" she cheers while taking it and skimming its pages. So she can touch things.

"It was down on the bookshelf in the storeroom," I explain.

"Oh, that makes sense. The secret part of the house," she reasons for herself.

"I am sorry for reading a bit of it," I realize that diaries are personal.

"It doesn't really matter anymore," she waves me off, "I am long dead."

"Still, I think there might be something to be said about respect for the dead," I at least feel awkward now. I mean she's right there!

"That's kind for you to say," she replies.

There is a clicking noise—that's a gun!

"Father is coming tonight it seems," Elizabeth comments with a weary sigh.

"I don't think he likes me," I say as I get my stuff ready.

"Oh, he doesn't like anyone anymore," she agrees before asking, "Now what?"

I cock my own weapon—useless for ghosts, but it's comforting. I tell her, "I plan to hide."

"Secret passage?" she suggests.

I nod as I barricade the door to the library with a chair. Now returning to the bench I lift up the hatch.

I get down the ladder fast and Elizabeth follows. She closes the hatch behind her.

Now in relative safety, I have to ask, "How are you able to interact with physical objects?"

"Good question. I cannot pass through them, so I have to touch them," she answers while helping me move the bookcase.

"So that might make you some sort of poltergeist?" I suggest.

"I don't think I feed off of the psychic energy of unstable teens," she replies. How does she know that? I look at her for an explanation and she adds, "I read over the last two's shoulders, they took a lot of notes. Especially the boy."

"Ah," I note, "You are quite knowledgeable," I tell her.

"People often left stuff behind when fleeing in terror. I can read instruction manuals and books. I even figured out how to use one of those VCR contraptions and video games. The future has some neat things," she points out.

"Well if I survive this you can check out some of the latest gear," I tell her. Having a ghost for a friend would certainly make life interesting.

"I will take you up on that offer," she says as we enter the basement of the burned carriage house. Elizabeth inspecting the wreckage observes, "The lift is out."

"Stairs are of course rotted," I put my foot on the first one to only watch it crack. I didn't even put my weight on it!

"You can't fly, can you?" I ask.

"Tried a while back. It did not end well," she tells me.

"Let me guess, you tried from the balcony?" I ask while looking around for something I could use to climb.

"Yeah, the fall hurt for a bit," she confesses.

Wait, "Hurt? I thought ghosts couldn't feel physical pain?" Now I am confused.

"Other than myself and my parents, I've never encountered any other real ghosts. The pain is unpleasant, but it goes away quickly and it won't kill me. I know books tell us ghosts can't feel pain, but that seem to be a fictional presumption in my experience," she says while looking up.

"Good point. I can't say I have actually encountered other ghosts," I agree as I decide climbing is a bad idea. The rocks are too smooth, or moss-covered to try that. Plus, who knows what that moss is. I sigh as I can feel my tennis shoes soak through. It's cold, damp, and smells funny down here.

"Well, I think you should be at least safe down here from Father," Elizabeth concludes.

"Sure, I am glad for that. Though, I wish I had grabbed a jacket," I can't help but shiver. This sweater is too light. I will take discomfort over death, but I'm still going to complain.

"I remember how cold it was. I mean I don't really feel it now, but I grew up in New York and spent some time south of the Mason-Dixon line before here," she says to me.

"I came from the Atlanta area, so this is awful," I say as I take a seat on one of the stairs that seems a bit less rotted and molded than the one I tried.

"Oh, I spent some time there," she comments, "Bit more humid than to my liking."

"Well it was all I knew. Nothing there was paranormal. Just school, video games, exercise and chores. My life was utterly unremarkable. This move has upended everything I have thought about my life and the world. That was before I discovered I was in a haunted house." I say leaning back and trying to get comfortable. The steps creak a ton. This one though should work as a seat.

Elizabeth leaning against the wall across from me says, "Well, my life was very mundane at least until I started traveling. Did you ever travel much?"

"Not really much," I confess, "My parents didn't really have the urge to go far with me until they decided to come out here."

"I wound up here because my father thought striking out West would reinvigorate him. He was an adventurer at heart and as they say now on TV, probably suffering a mid-life crisis," she replies.

"That fits what I have read about him—businessman, soldier and avid hunter," I recall the Society's research.

"This house meant more to him than my mother. This was his paradise in the Wilderness, but my mother's social exiled hell," Elizabeth says.

"New York is a lively place," I reason. Everything happens there, "I hadn't heard of this place until the move came up."

"Back then nobody seemed to be out here other than cowboys, homesteaders, cavalrymen and Indians," she tells me.

"There's still not a lot of people out here," I point out.

That gets her laughing. "Some things never change!" she tells me. Her laughter is light and fits her ethereal form.

"Well we're here, that means something," I state.

She laughs even more at that, "We may not have 'proper society,' but ghosts count for something!"

"Too bad your parents couldn't have a better attitude about it," I state.

"They are hardly my parents now. Those two literally and metaphorically died long ago," she has a distant look, "The Mother and Father that attack now only have their likeness and some of their mannerisms."

"I'm sorry."

"No, I periodically forget that when I see them. You'd think I learn better. Their blind hatred and violence are even sometimes against me if I get in their way. They leave me alone when I play the piano," she confesses.

I feel exhaustion set in. I am tired and cold. Hiding down

in this rotting hole doesn't solve the mystery. I have the information from the Society, my own findings and memories, but I just cannot make heads or tails of the whole thing. All the facts and evidence are a jumble in my tired head.

I look over at Elizabeth as she now sits on a rotted, broken crate. She's lost in thought too. Her unworldly form glows in the total darkness. She is the only light source other than my flashlight. To her, I guess, people come and go. But she remains all the same.

How does she not go mad from all this? Her parents in some way make more sense. They've clearly shed their humanity. Why has she kept hers?

CHAPTER 20: FIFTH DAY

Dripping on my wet forehead gets me to wake up. I tumble into some muddy slop in the confusion. Damn! It feels slimly and moist—ick!

Picking myself up, I realize I must have fallen asleep under the ruins of the carriage house. Given the damp conditions, that may take a few years off my life. At that realization, I hastily wipe off the muck. That smears it in more than anything.

What time is it? I pull out my cellphone to find—of course it's dead. The thing spent the night searching for a signal in what amounts to a concrete bunker. It figures.

Somewhere above I think I hear a car horn! Hopefully it is the Scipio twins and their cousin. If it is them, then it is morning. It means I made it through the fourth night!

It's a struggle, but I clamber out of the secret passage and back into the library. The room, although chaotic in the moving process, is now even worse. Mr. Easton overturned most of the boxes. He took out his immortal rage out on our stuff. Mom and Dad are going to be pissed.

Now the doorbell rings. I get over the spilled boxes and head for the front door. This house is a ruin, though now is not the time to address that problem.

I open the door and find the familiar Scipione twins and an unfamiliar girl their age. The cousin, I guess. They drove up in a mud drenched jeep. However, they are all cleanly dressed in cargo pants and t-shirts.

"Glad to see you alive this time," Danna states.

"Well, I'm glad I made it this far," I agree before asking, "How are you three so clean?" I gesture towards their car. It's dripping with slush.

"Coveralls," Cassandra explains, I see the muck covered suits are draped over the side of the car.

"We do not always remember them though," Danna adds.

"Good idea when remembered. Well, come on in," I invite them inside, "Was it hard to get here?"

"Damn—it was fun!" their cousin states. She is about the same height as Cassandra, but much, I guess, tougher looking.

"Ah this is our cousin, Antonia Scipio. As for our trip. It took a couple hours. We only had to really dig out of a big mess once," Cassandra replies, then elbowing Antonia she adds, "Someone underestimated the depth of a snow and mud pile."

"A pleasure to meet you Antonia, I am Henry Torrington," I say as we gather in the entryway.

"How was your evening?" Danna asks as he notes my roughed-up state.

"I started the evening well enough. I read through Elizabeth's diary of her travels before she came here. Then the ghost herself visited me," I explain leading them towards the library.

"I've read the reports. Elizabeth seems nice," Antonia comments while looking around the entry.

"She's a lifesaver too. Mr. Easton then forced me to spend a night under the carriage house. He was on the hunt," I tell them.

"That's more aggressive for that night," he ponders before asking, "Did you just get out?" We pause in front of the library door. They can all see the carnage of that room from the hall.

"Yes, it's awful down there—damp and cold," I reply.

"You want a shower and breakfast before we spelunk back down there?" Cassandra asks.

"Actually, yeah," I admit. I know I must smell as terrible as I feel. And then my stomach growls.

"Well, you get the shower. We brought some stuff in the car for breakfast," Cassandra takes charge.

"I'll make sure the jeep is ready for a departure," Antonia

states finding her own job.

"Alright, that would all help," I reply as I turn to head upstairs.

About halfway up, Danna calls up, "Find something long sleeved. When we start poking around down there who knows what's there. We'll be using masks and gloves as well."

Not comforting. I pause and ask, "Do I need to worry about mold or the cold from a night down there?"

Cassandra, about to head out the front door says, "Hopefully no?"

That does not sound reassuring, then she adds, "If you feel sick, we'll get you help."

"Great," I do not feel reassured beyond being certain I will make it to a hospital with their help.

For now, a hot shower and plenty of antibacterial soap might be the best I can do!

* * *

The blissful shower cleared my mind and body. I now feel like a decent human being again. I dig out some old jeans and a long sleeve shirt I don't care too much for. Given we're going back down there again, I assume I'll shower again today.

Coming back downstairs I overhear the Scipione family talking in the kitchen. Though the smells of bacon, coffee and scrambled eggs are enticing, I hold back in the hall. I want to hear what they have to say when I am not around.

"So, you don't have any ideas on solving this Cass. Well what about you Danna?" Antonia asks.

"We've gotten a ton on new information on the house and its mystery this time. Torrington has done wonders—but," he trails off.

"But not enough," Cassandra finishes his sentence.

"Information does not directly mean answers. We have a ton of pieces, but no idea how the pieces fit," Danna explains.

"So, our best bet is to get him out of here. If we cannot figure this out, then Walpurgisnacht would be a death sentence," Cassandra states before adding, "I don't think even with combined forces we'd succeed."

"I don't know. The anniversary of the Easton's deaths might be the only time to solve the mystery. You know the solving of the mystery should be the climax of the story," Antonia disagrees in a way that worries me. This is my real life, not fiction!

"You think this is a classic haunting mystery or horror?" Cassandra seems to be entertaining the idea. No!

"Well, one of us needs to be the optimist," Antonia counters.

"Well, evidence shows that the few that survived did so at the cost of sanity. The records at Yankton's asylum show that," Danna points out.

"Yeah, so? What do you mean?" Antonia replies. I can feel the annoyance in her voice from up here.

"What he's saying is we might be guessing the wrong genre. You think mystery. I think horror. Danna here thinks Lovecraftian horror. You know, knowledge of the truth is directly proportional to the madness," Cassandra explains.

"Huh, I hadn't considered that," Antonia replies. Now they're on genres. I don't think they have much to say behind my back. I think I can trust them.

At this point, I decide to enter, "Something smells wonderful," I comment.

"'Be prepared' is a good motto," Danna muses as Cassandra pans everything up.

Moving to the dining room, I ask, "I hope you stayed out of the main fridge."

"Nice bio-weapon you're hiding there. Does the League of Nations or the EPA know?" Antonia comments with a wince.

"Several weeks ago, that might have been Chinese food. Too bad we can't beat ghosts with it," I admit.

"Indeed," Danna agrees.

Getting into the eggs I can't help but praise, "This is wonderful," I tell them. Had they thrown in some biscuits and gravy it would be like a weekend breakfast that Mom and Dad would make.

We eat for a bit and then Danna starts, "Cassandra and I are still bitter over not solving this mystery. You found some great stuff, but we don't have things figured out yet."

"Well there's still a lot to go through still," I point out before having some coffee, "You haven't had a chance to review what I just found."

"We are making progress. I won't deny that," Danna agrees.

Seeing that we probably then won't solve this mystery over breakfast, I want to find more about them. So, I ask, "Where are you coming in from Antonia?"

"I lived here until about a year ago. My parents moved down to Colorado, to some town north of Denver," she answers.

"She misses us," Cassandra teases, but they seem like it's all in good humor.

"Family is foundation," Danna chimes in.

"Plus, we do all the cool stuff up here," Antonia says fondly before adding, "I too was a member of the Society."

"Neat, what part of the book did you contribute to?" I ask.

"I was a part of the search for a lost mine. The one we actually found," she boasts. Antonia has a beaming smile.

"I'll have to read the rest of the book," I decide.

"Now we'll have to update the book," Cassandra says looking over to Antonia, "The Society may have lost public and parental support, but we haven't stopped research. You can't ban kids from reading books or poking around archives in America at least."

"Oh, is the Society President ready to reactivate things?" Danna asks.

"The call of adventure and mystery is one that either pushes you on or makes you choose to chase it for the rest of your life. Thanks to Torrington here, we have new developments on this story," Cassandra explains.

"Does that mean we will be getting more help?" I really

hope we are getting more assistance.

"No one besides Antonia unfortunately," Cassandra states, "Technically we cannot be here. The police are keeping tabs on the movements of most of our group."

"Antonia is useful though," Danna points out.

"True, she is a good driver, great shot and tough," Cassandra adds.

Antonia flattered at her cousins' praise says, "Come on you two! The four of us together are probably the best team to solve this! We got Henry here—he won't die and finds great stuff, I can be the muscle, Cass here is the smartest, and Danna here is always up to something that will make all the difference!"

"I just hope we can get it right this time," I reply as we finish up breakfast.

Cleanup is a breeze with four people. Returning to the hall, I now notice the gear they brought along. Danna opens a large plastic wheeled trunk to reveal all kinds of equipment—lots of army surplus: rope, big sheathed knives. I think that might be a homemade Geiger counter. It's something cobbled together out of old electronics.

"Right, so we'll start with sanitation gear. Each of us will need a mask and gloves," Cassandra explains while handing us each a gas mask.

Antonia shows me how to put on a mask while Danna digs out some digital cameras and a small remote-control quadcopter drone with a tablet screen control pad. These guys must be quite rich too. I am also given an LED headlamp.

Cassandra pulls out a white backpack with a cord and attached is what looks kind of like a microphone.

I put on my gas mask and discover I do not feel as cool as I think I should look in one of these things. It is hard to see and breathing through a filter is a bit more work than I am used to. It tastes a bit chalky—I hope that's normal. Then with vinyl gloves and headlamp on, I am ready to go. This feels weird. I hope we don't actually need all of this. I spent a whole night down there!

It's a bit muffled, but Danna says, "Can everybody hear me?"

"You bet," Cassandra and Antonia answer in muffled unison.

"Yes," I reply.

"Good, lead the way then," Cassandra requests.

"Right this way," I speak up a bit to make sure I'm heard.

As we pass through the secret passage, Cassandra comments, "I guess Mr. Easton doesn't know his own house too well."

"Or he couldn't follow?" Antonia points out.

"But Elizabeth followed me. She was under the carriage house with me during the haunting hours," I state.

"Weird," is all Danna has to say on the matter.

Cassandra whistles at the sight of the storeroom lit up by our flashlights and says, "Well, we did not know about this before."

"I thought Mr. Easton built the place," Antonia states as Cassandra takes some pictures. Meanwhile Danna's drone zips around taking some pictures too.

"No, no he commissioned an architect and ex-rail workers to build it. He might not have known all the details. Plus, the blueprints went missing in his lifetime," Danna states without looking up from his tablet computer.

"Look at this tunnel though. How can anyone build that and not talk about it afterwards? I mean like the construction worker comes home and tells his wife, 'Like we just built this huge ass secret tunnel that you can run a carriage through under this rich guy's house,'" Antonia counters.

"The workers were Chinese that came directly over from mainland China. They built the railroad, a couple other things and left—mostly sent or deported back." Danna points out.

"Oh," that explanation sounds reasonable.

"Let's check out the tunnel and basement of the carriage house first," Cassandra orders.

"Even still how do you lose track of all this stuff?" Danna asks gesturing.

"Well Elizabeth knew about it," I point out, "Though I don't know if she was alive when she found out."

"The servants had to have known about this," Danna decides.

"Well, somebody got all the stuff down here," I point out as we reach the basement of the carriage house.

Danna's drone turns on an LED lantern which lights up much of the room. It then flies up scanning the higher parts we cannot reach.

"So, what should we be looking for?" I ask.

"Not sure. The storeroom might tell us more given the decayed state of this place," Cassandra concludes.

"In here—anything would help. You said you found the diary in the storeroom?" Danna asks for clarification.

"Yeah, on the bookshelf that the tunnel is hidden behind," I answer looking around. Through the gas mask, it is harder to see, but I feel a bit safer. Though this is a bit stuffy.

I head into the center of the room to inspect what must have been some sort of elevator. I can see the remains of some sort of pulley system. It is pretty clear that this was how they filled the storeroom.

"Cassandra how's the air? My mask is stuffy," Antonia whines.

"It's," she waves her wand/microphone sensor thing at an odd clump of moss. She waits a second while checking a readout on the device, "It's okay. Air is fine, keep those gloves on though. I'll be collecting some mold samples."

Good. We then all pull off the uncomfortable things. Antonia meanwhile cheers, "Great!"

"In the bag," Danna calls as Cassandra throws hers at him. Antonia follows suit and I do also. He adds them to his backpack.

Returning back to work, I take a picture with my cellphone of the remaining elevator mechanisms before moving on. For what feels like an eternity we look around this empty, messy, moldy, damp ruin.

"This isn't working," Danna finally decides as he lands his drone on his hand.

"Your drone see anything?" Cassandra asks.

"Other than a drained battery? No," he answers while switching out the battery with another in his backpack.

"Should we move to the storeroom?" I suggest.

"Might as well. We can't find anything here," Antonia agrees.

"Alright, let's do that," Cassandra concedes.

Stepping out of the basement, Danna collects all of our gloves into a biohazard bag and hands us cloth booties and a new pair of gloves. "For the furniture," he explains.

"So, what might we be looking for in here?" I ask. I feel like we also need magnify glasses with all this detective work.

"If we are lucky, some sort of diary. Ideally the sequel to the one you found," Cassandra states. You can hear the tinge of jealousy in her tone, "You've had the best luck in that regard. We were not able to find anything that old in our initial research of this place."

"My group found a diary that ultimately got us to the lost mine," Antonia brags.

As I start on the bookshelf with Danna, I ask, "How operational is the Society now?" They sound like they are planning to make a comeback.

"Very operational. Some members are preparing a new publication on some local stories found throughout the area. We cannot operate in public doing fieldwork, but our members have a backlog of research to carry out anyways," Danna answers as he takes a book off the shelf.

"What's that?" I ask him.

"Looks like a French lesson workbook of some sort," Danna comments as he turns through the pages, "There are a lot of annotations in here. It's probably nothing, but we ought to go through it."

"Who knows, Elizabeth might have written something other than class notes," I suggest.

"Hopefully," Danna agrees before calling over, "Cassandra, French textbook notes for us to translate."

"Sure," she calls back while inspecting what appears to be a desk in the corner.

Antonia comments, "How much you willing to bet there is a secret compartment in that desk Cassandra?"

"Probably, though it likely will have only Mr. Easton's ledger. That might be interesting to look at," she replies.

"You think their deaths might involve money?" I ask.

"Rich people problems could be a cause," Danna states.

"Exactly. And we still don't have a cause for their deaths. I don't think it randomly happened," Cassandra agrees.

We continue to search around with no major finds. I learned to pull dust covers off slowly though. I thought that dust cloud from the pool table was going to kill me!

After some time, Antonia finally protests, "Ugh, this is nothing like the movies!"

"Fictional murder mysteries are concise. All the pieces can be found and fitted together," I agree. This is frustrating. I want to solve this mystery and play pool. I presume that by owning the house I get all this cool loot!

"We keep finding pieces, but who knows if they are all for the jigsaw puzzle, we are assembling," Danna adds with despair.

"Maybe we should break for lunch. Hunger leads to frustration," Cassandra decides. I hadn't realized how much time had passed! Giving up for now, we retreat for the kitchen.

CHAPTER 21: WALPURGISNACHT

A rumble of a car engine and bump on the road wakes me up.

"Whoa, you passed out there," Cassandra comments. I reawaken finding myself riding into town in the Scipione jeep. I was in the middle of a rather vivid dream.

"I dozed off," I excuse myself, "Moving, ghosts, etc. these things are tiring."

"True," Danna agrees.

"Do you guys think you'll ever solve the mystery of the Easton Estate?" Antonia asks as she drives at speeds that make me glad I have a seatbelt. This is a dirt road, not a NASCAR track! It's getting dark too!

Cassandra comments, "Well we won't fail through a lack of trying. Tonight's another chance."

"Don't worry, we'll keep trying. You know—try, try and try again," Danna adds.

"Well that can wait. I cannot wait for the bonfire!" Antonia chimes in. Somehow, she is able to drive in this slop formerly known as a road. She has a good pair of eyes and steady hands at the wheel.

I feel optimistic. We can do this! Research and experience will eventually triumph. Each time we get closer and closer. I conclude, "We will solve it."

CHAPTER 22: A SIXTH DAY...

I open my eyes. Pain tells me that I'm not dead. Light streams into the house. It must be morning. I'm in the entryway, near the conservatory, left propped up against the wall. Somehow, I survived Walpurgisnacht alone this time.

Looking at my body, I find it beaten, bruised and bloody. The exact "how I'm still alive explanation" escapes me. That's all my blood staining the place. In the last fight I was the only human. Not fair. I think, I might die. I sag, feeling heavy.

Exhausted, I can't do a whole lot more. Elizabeth clearly attempted some first aid. It looks like she tried bandaging my wounds with some towels. But the improvised bandages are blood soaked. I am certain I was shot at least once too.

I think I hear a car pull up. I hope that's not my parents. I love them, but neither are prepared for the carnage or helping me. They're bad with handling emergencies.

It sounds like the car slides to a stop out front on the gravel driveway. Good, not them, my parents don't drive recklessly like that. Cops then? No. There's no way they'd be here by now. The road up is too awful for them. Damn weather.

There's a loud car horn honk, though I don't hear too well. Exchanging gunfire isn't great for my hearing.

Then over a megaphone someone calls, "Hello, this is the Scipione Family. You alive in there Torrington!?" It's Cassandra!

"Not dead yet!" I yell as loud as I can with my hoarse throat. I'm thirsty.

I hear the sounds of their feet on the porch. There's a rattling of the door handle before another call from the megaphone, "Your door's locked!"

"Damn it!" I yell back.

"You near the door?" an unrecognizable though, it does seem familiar, voice asks. A girl—maybe their cousin Antonia? They've mentioned her before.

"Near the conservatory!" I yell back. My throat is getting sore from all this plus nearly being strangled. Turns out Mrs. Easton can throw that noose like a damn cowboy.

"Good, cover your ears," she yells back. Then there's a pump of a shotgun.

Danna and Cassandra start to protest in stereo, "Are you sure this is a good—"

They are interrupted by a shotgun blast that rattles the doors before they're kicked inwards. The wood and hinges cracking at the impact. Weren't those meant to open outwards?

In storms a girl dressed in military surplus, she wears shooting earmuffs and safety glasses. Over one eye she wears a gray eyepatch. This girl has an almost feral grin on her face. She ejects a spent casing from her shotgun and sweeps the room. Then comments, "I'm fine you two! I needed this!"

Then seeing me she says, "Though I can't say the same for this gentleman."

Danna and Cassandra follow in. Like typical twins, they wear matching safari suits and shooting safety gear. Though Danna carries a laptop and Cassandra thankfully carries a very large first aid kit.

Seeing me, Cassandra rushes over while pulling on surgical gloves. I can see in her eyes that I am not in good condition. Her medical expertise at least rivals, if not surpasses mine. Her fast-moving eyes scan my body. She's trying to figure out where to start on my beaten body.

While she sets to that task, Danna sits next to me. Opening up his laptop and asks me, "Let her work, now tell me what happened?"

"Where do I start?" I ask after a drink of water offered by Cassandra. I take small sips to prevent coughing. The cold-water washes wonderfully over my dry throat.

"Did you win, or did you just survive?" Antonia calls over, she seems to be poking her way through the carnage with the barrel of her gun. She looks almost like a soldier.

"Survive, I didn't solve the mystery or beat them. I just managed to not die before the clock ended the haunting hour," as I tell her. I do know that much. I can feel some of my strength return. Water is wonderful.

"Did you do anything to the clock?" Danna asks as he types. He doesn't seem too concerned, so I must be doing better that I thought.

"No," I tell him. Cassandra must be a miracle worker. Ratcheting through my wounds, she methodically cleans and redresses with a fast, yet controlled urgency. I might survive yet.

"I see," Danna comments as he works. He's got everyone else handling the immediate situation.

Contributing my own theory to the big picture, I tell him, "I am certain the clock is the power source or something."

"I guess," Danna ponders, "Broken clock, broken family. It works when they haunt, not when they aren't."

"So, destroy it?" I suggest. I feel faint, but I think I've solved it.

Cassandra pauses her work and says something I can't understand. He nods with a steeled expression.

Then addressing me he says, "We could destroy it at this time. If anything, it is likely a major variable."

"Yes, destroy it now!" I order, gathering more strength than I thought I had.

He nods again and says, "Antonia. Clock in the living room, what will it take?"

She walks over there and asks, "We need the mechanical parts busted right?"

"Yes, the mechanism mostly, I don't think the frame matters," he answers.

"Give Torrington earplugs," she calls back.

Cassandra pulls out a pair of earmuffs and shooting glasses from the bag and puts them on me before resuming first aid.

"Range ready," Danna calls.

"Slug round, steel, firing for effect," is Antonia's reply before firing a shot. It sounds so distant between the muffs and my recent hearing loss.

Antonia apparently isn't satisfied, and the old grandfather clock is knocked over into the entry. It hits the ground with several off-key chimes. She ejects the spent shell and fires again. The blast sends chunks of wood flying and the bells in it chime again.

That doesn't seem to work, so she puts the safety of her gun on and leans it against the wall. Storming out of the house, she then comes back with an ax and sledgehammer.

Danna gets up saying to me, "I'm sure you'd join in if you could." He takes the hammer from Antonia. With her leading, she swings down and puts a deep crack in the frame. Danna swings the hammer overhead and smashes it down on the back of the ax blade ramming it into the frame with a loud crack. A few gears and clock parts come out and roll across the floor.

Antonia wretches the blade out and the two proceed to chop and smash the old clock with a methodical motion of steel and muscle. Those two are ruthless. That mass of busted gears, wood and glass doesn't even look like it was ever a clock.

Cassandra ignores her destructive sibling and cousin and continues her work. Mom and Dad are going to be furious, but those ghosts had to be stopped. I just wish that Elizabeth didn't have to suffer as well. By herself, her haunting would be a pleasant addition to this big house.

As they finish, Cassandra says, "I think you're stable enough to move. Are you two done?"

"At this time, yes," Danna decides as Antonia lands the final blow.

"Great, fetch me the stretcher," Cassandra orders. Antonia pulls out the ax with a creaking of wood and bell chimes.

"Of course, Cass," he answers as he takes the ax from Antonia and steps out.

I finally feel like I can relax...well for now. We still haven't figured this mystery out. It's not over, even now Something makes me think that. But. But, I'll keep trying.

AFTERWORD

Thank you for purchasing this book. I do hope you've enjoyed it.

During the closed world created by COVID-19, I found myself with a considerable amount of time to finally finish this book. Originally, I had intended to publish this last year, but felt it needed more editing. This particular work is my most challenging publication yet! It's the longest thing I have written and the most complicated.

Here's the tale of how this story came to be. The first writing of *Easton Estate* came out of a challenge I made for myself back in college. I wanted to see if I could write a novel (well the original draft was more of a novelette) in one sitting (with bathroom breaks of course.) I started late at night and through the power of coffee, I drafted. Staining my hands with purple ink, I toiled and wrote. For some odd reason, I had included in the challenge the use of a dip pen. It was one of those more decorative than functional ones, a Romanov Bronze Stylus. In hindsight, I should have not started the challenge after playing a round of bar trivia with some of my colleagues.

Anyways, to this day, I am not sure how long the first draft took. Being that it was summer, I didn't need to contact anyone for a few days. Tired and drained after all that time, I think it was daylight, I went to sleep for five or six hours. So in the disoriented fallout, there's no logged start or finish time.

The challenge is probably why editing took so long. In the editing process, I dramatically lengthened the story and rewrote Elizabeth's character. I also fleshed out some aspects of Henry too. Oh well, I enjoyed both the challenge and fixing the mess it made!

Anyways, I do hope you keep a look out for my future works! I inconsistently maintain an author page at https://drlhicks.word-press.com.

Until Later,

D.R.L. Hicks

ABOUT THE AUTHOR

D. R. L. Hicks

D.R.L. Hicks is someone who has little to say about one's self. There's a joy of writing, reading, travel, and enjoying life. The fellow has also written Upon the Isle of Serenity: A Collection of Three Adventures which is an anthology of previous published eBooks. Resides on planet Earth.

BOOKS BY THIS AUTHOR

Lost Upon The Isle Of Serenity: A Collection Of Adventures

He wakes up with no memory of his identity. His supposed sisters want to go to a lighthouse. (Spoiler alert: the lighthouse is closed.)
And...
Anna doesn't know dreams from reality. Given the dangers, that could be problematic for a girl in over her head.

Blair's Beginning

Blaire is at a loss. One day this young woman just finds herself standing before a mirror. No memory of who she is, why she got there, or what she was doing prior. Her current name came from a clipboard!